Samuel French Acting

The Keen Collection
One-Acts by Contemporary Playwrights
Volume 5

Rat Court
by Boo Killebrew

Tilda Swinton Betrayed Us
by A. Rey Pamatmat

And Action
by Eleanor Burgess

SAMUELFRENCH.COM   SAMUELFRENCH.CO.UK

Rat Court Copyright © 2018 by Boo Killebrew
Tilda Swinton Betrayed Us Copyright © 2018 by A. Rey Pamatmat
And Action Copyright © 2018 by Eleanor Burgess
All Rights Reserved

THE KEEN COLLECTION: VOLUME 5 is fully protected under the copyright laws of the United States of America, the British Commonwealth, including Canada, and all member countries of the Berne Convention for the Protection of Literary and Artistic Works, the Universal Copyright Convention, and/or the World Trade Organization conforming to the Agreement on Trade Related Aspects of Intellectual Property Rights. All rights, including professional and amateur stage productions, recitation, lecturing, public reading, motion picture, radio broadcasting, television and the rights of translation into foreign languages are strictly reserved.

ISBN 978-0-573-70669-1

www.SamuelFrench.com
www.SamuelFrench.co.uk

FOR PRODUCTION ENQUIRIES

UNITED STATES AND CANADA
Info@SamuelFrench.com
1-866-598-8449

UNITED KINGDOM AND EUROPE
Plays@SamuelFrench.co.uk
020-7255-4302

Each title is subject to availability from Samuel French, depending upon country of performance. Please be aware that *THE KEEN COLLECTION: VOLUME 5* may not be licensed by Samuel French in your territory. Professional and amateur producers should contact the nearest Samuel French office or licensing partner to verify availability.

CAUTION: Professional and amateur producers are hereby warned that *THE KEEN COLLECTION: VOLUME 5* is subject to a licensing fee. Publication of this play(s) does not imply availability for performance. Both amateurs and professionals considering a production are strongly advised to apply to Samuel French before starting rehearsals, advertising, or booking a theater. A licensing fee must be paid whether the title(s) is presented for charity or gain and whether or not admission is charged. Professional/Stock licensing fees are quoted upon application to Samuel French.

No one shall make any changes in this title(s) for the purpose of production. No part of this book may be reproduced, stored in a retrieval system, or transmitted in any form, by any means, now known or yet to be invented, including mechanical, electronic, photocopying, recording, videotaping, or otherwise, without the prior written permission of the publisher. No one shall upload this title(s), or part of this title(s), to any social media websites.

For all enquiries regarding motion picture, television, and other media rights, please contact Samuel French.

MUSIC USE NOTE

Licensees are solely responsible for obtaining formal written permission from copyright owners to use copyrighted music in the performance of this play and are strongly cautioned to do so. If no such permission is obtained by the licensee, then the licensee must use only original music that the licensee owns and controls. Licensees are solely responsible and liable for all music clearances and shall indemnify the copyright owners of the play(s) and their licensing agent, Samuel French, against any costs, expenses, losses and liabilities arising from the use of music by licensees. Please contact the appropriate music licensing authority in your territory for the rights to any incidental music.

IMPORTANT BILLING AND CREDIT REQUIREMENTS

If you have obtained performance rights to this title, please refer to your licensing agreement for important billing and credit requirements.

TABLE OF CONTENTS

About Keen Teens 7

Keen Teens Angels 9

Rat Court 11

Tilda Swinton Betrayed Us 43

And Action 71

ABOUT KEEN TEENS

Keen Company is an award-winning Off-Broadway theater producing stories about the decisive moments since 2000. The cornerstone of the company's outreach and educational efforts is Keen Teens. The program improves the quality of plays written for high school students by commissioning scripts from accomplished New York City playwrights. This free program for students provides invaluable mentorship opportunities – working alongside professional writers, directors, and designers to rehearse and premiere new work.

When first creating Keen Teens in 2007, the company found that teachers did not have access to material that was intended for a high school stage. Educators were left with either presenting classic plays never designed for teen actors, or producing simple skits that lacked rich material relevant to modern students. Central to Keen Company's mission is to produce theatre that patrons can identify with and connect to, however no such material existed for students and educators. Keen Teens brings the company's values to the high school stage by developing new work tailored specifically to be relevant and engaging to teen actors and audiences.

Keen Teens commissions and presents work that speaks to teens on their level, creating work that is as complex and multilayered as the high school world. Form, style, and context vary amongst each playwright and season. Topics have included cyberbullying and teen suicide (*Why Aren't You Dead Already?* by Halley Feiffer), same-sex relationships amongst athletes (*Going Left* by Kristoffer Diaz), environmental concerns (*A Polar Bear in New Jersey* by Anna Moench), death within a family (*Syd Arthur* by Kenny Finkle), and even the perils of YouTube fame (*30 Million* by Max Vernon and Jason Kim). All pieces deal honestly and provocatively with their subject matter – some through comedy and farce, some through sincerity and intimate portraits.

As well as being tailored to the social and emotional world of teens, each piece is also designed to be accessible to educators and drama festivals. Commissions consist of thirty-minute plays, simple designs, large casts, and flexible genders. These requirements are designed so that high schools might include as many students as possible and present their productions on their own, in an evening, or as part of a competition.

Every year the Keen Teens program culminates in the world premiere performances of three newly commissioned one-act plays at the Lion Theatre in Theater Row, New York City. Since

2005, Keen Teens has made possible the Off-Broadway debut of over three hundred young actors and has led to the publication of over twenty-five new one-act plays. Not only are these plays regularly produced in the United States, but in various countries around the world, from Australia to Singapore.

For more information, please visit *www.keencompany.org/teens*.

KEEN TEENS ANGELS 2016-2017

42nd St. Development Corp., Lindsay Adkins, Joanne Ainsworth, Sarah Alexander, Cathy & Robert Altholz, Howard Balaban, Grace Beggins, Amy & Brad Ball, Jeffery & Tina Bolton, Bill & Casey Bradford, Blake & Josh Bradford, Karen Bradford, Sara Brandston, Paul Brill, Kathleen Chalfant, Buena Chilstrom, Maria Cicio, Gary & Ellen Cohen, Michael Coratolo, Elizabeth Corradino, Rose Courtney, Alexander Coxe, Michael Cristofer, Katherine Crost, Michela Daliana, Joanna D'Angelo, Lucy & Nathaniel Day, Joseph Deasy, Marie DiSalvo, Emily Donahoe, Linda D'Onofrio, Maralène Downs, Mary Durante, Tony Fingleton, Kenny Finkle, Cathy Frankel, Sharon Friedland, Patricia Follert, Jack & Ann Gilpin, Douglas Giombarrese, Greg Graham, Timothy Grandia, José Gutierrez, Benjamin Goldberg, Sylvia Golden, Barbara McIntyre Hack, Richard & Edith Hanley, Daoud Heidami, Erin Hogan, Victoria Leacock Hoffman, Monica Lewinsky, Kimberly Howard, Sally & Robert Huxley, Stephen Kantor, David & Kate Kies, Jae Kim, Judith S. Lidsky, Kevin & Jana Maher, Marsha Mason, David McMahon, Madeline Marzano-Lesnevich, Andrew Miltenberg, Cynthia & Bruce Miltenberg, Nancy Morgan, Jasmine Nielsen, Marianna Noto, Matt O'Grady, Joy Pak, Merrill & Martin Pavane, David & Faith Pedowitz, David & Katherine Rabinowitz, Ulga Staffen, Rhonda Pohl, Rebecca Randall, Diana Roitman, Nanny Lee Russell, Betsy & Norman Samet, Jim Spare, Ron Schwartz, Pamela Thomas, Louis Viel, Les Waters, Louly & Bill Williams, Alban Wilson, Marie & Alan Wolpert, Ernest & Judith Wong, Angela Reed & Todd Cerveris, Jeffrey Blair & Ivor Clark, Mia Dillon & Keir Dullea, Pat Stockhausen & Mike Emmerman, Rhonda Paul & Mark Feldman, Charles Snipes & Robert Furlong, Roberta Greenberg & Robert Goldy, Kathy Chazen & Larry Miller, Susan Shapiro & Bob Piller, David Ehrich & Chris Shyer, Vincent Smith & Alice Silkworth

RAT COURT

Boo Killebrew

RAT COURT premiered May 13, 2017 at the Lion Theatre at Theatre Row in New York City. The performance was directed by Daisy Walker. The cast was as follows:

SUNNY	Alonnie Johnson
NAOMI	SaCha Stewart-Coleman
EMILY	Emerson Thomas-Gregory
MANDY	Jaylene Gonzalez
NATALIE	Tashi Everett
DE'SHAY	Roza Chervinsky
JULIE	Madelyn De Los Santos
M.K.	Pamela Guerrero
CULLEN	Giovanni Santalucia
SETH	Jaylen Key

CHARACTERS

SUNNY – F, sixteen

NAOMI – F, sixteen

EMILY – F, sixteen

MANDY – F, seventeen

NATALIE – F, seventeen

DE'SHAY – F, seventeen

JULIE – F, seventeen

M.K. – F, seventeen

CULLEN – M, seventeen

SETH – M, seventeen

TIME

The present. But we never see phones in this play.

Scene One

*(**SUNNY, EMILY,** and **NAOMI** in Emily's room. They each have a handbook.)*

EMILY. No makeup.

NAOMI. No bathing or washing your hair.

SUNNY. You have to wear whatever they make you to school.

NAOMI. No phones.

EMILY. For a week.

SUNNY. And if you don't have candy for them whenever they ask, you get a point ripped out. If you don't have the lyrics memorized to a Big Sister's favorite song when she commands you to belt it out, you get a point ripped out. You are able to earn points during park "activities" every day after school, the Tregg Throw –

EMILY. How do you earn points at the Tregg Throw? Don't they just hurl rotten eggs and trash at you?

NAOMI. Leslie said that when she was a Big Sister, the day before Tregg, they went behind the biology lab, to the dumpster where they threw out all the fetal pigs, you know, after the students had dissected them –

SUNNY. Wait. / Seriously?

NAOMI. And mixed them in all the garbage that they threw at the girls.

EMILY. But how do you earn points?

NAOMI. You get points if you don't throw up. And you can earn points at Rat Court.

EMILY. How?

NAOMI. Don't cry.

SUNNY. I bet they're gonna scream at me about Chris Beatty's party during Rat Court.

NAOMI. Probably. I wonder what we're gonna be. You know, the theme.

EMILY. I heard it was cows.

SUNNY. I heard it was Elvises.

NAOMI. Elvises? Like, Elvis Presley?

SUNNY. Yeah.

EMILY. That's fun.

NAOMI. I hope it's Elvises.

SUNNY. I hope Mandy is my Big Sis.

NAOMI. She will be.

EMILY. Julie is gonna pick you.

NAOMI. Probably.

EMILY. De'Shay said she had tabs on me.

SUNNY. What about the girls that nobody wants?

NAOMI. Leslie told me that when she was a Big Sister nobody wanted Johanna Pickard –

EMILY. Because of that stuff with her half-brother?

NAOMI. So Leslie ended up saying that she would split her.

SUNNY. What?

NAOMI. With two other Big Sisters.

EMILY. Really?

NAOMI. Leslie already had a Little Sister, Janet Urbina –

EMILY. Right.

NAOMI. So, she didn't want to have to buy all the stuff for two people, especially when she didn't even want Johanna in the first place.

SUNNY. Of course.

NAOMI. And they didn't want to tell Johanna that she couldn't rush, that nobody wanted her –

EMILY. Why?

NAOMI. What?

EMILY. Why didn't they just tell Johanna that nobody wanted her?

NAOMI. Because that's mean.

EMILY. But, you have to be asked to sign up for rush.

SUNNY. No, you don't.

NAOMI. Anybody can sign up for rush.

EMILY. No, that's not –

NAOMI. Well, anyone that thinks they can sign up can sign up.

EMILY. So, she didn't realize...? Didn't realize that...that this wasn't really...her group?

NAOMI. Right. Or, maybe she did. And signing up to rush was a way for her to get in that group. Like, a way to sneak into popularity.

EMILY. Oh.

NAOMI. Yeah. And I mean...no one is gonna tell her, like, "No." That's too mean.

EMILY. So she went through rush with three Big Sisters?

NAOMI. Yeah. And Leslie said that they ended up having a great time with Johanna.

SUNNY. That's awesome.

(Quiet.)

EMILY. What if no one wants me?

NAOMI. Em.

SUNNY. You said De'Shay told you she –

EMILY. That's what she said. But –

NAOMI. Em.

EMILY. She might not and –

NAOMI. Em.

EMILY. What?

NAOMI. You're not Johanna Pickard.

SUNNY. Do you think they'll be able to tell if I wear, like, just a tiny bit of concealer?

NAOMI. They're in the school parking lot every morning with face-wipes.

EMILY. Mandy is gonna make you wear the craziest shit. She's twisted.

SUNNY. I know.

      (A beat. Then the three girls smile.)

NAOMI. This is gonna be so fun.

Scene Two

(SUNNY and CULLEN in the school parking lot.)

SUNNY. So I ask, "Mom, where are you taking me?!"

CULLEN. Right.

SUNNY. She doesn't answer. And I'm like, "Mom, you just checked me out of school, I'm missing an important quiz, and you're not gonna tell me where we're going?" And she just keeps driving and doesn't say anything.

CULLEN. Okay...

SUNNY. And I say, "Mom! Where are you taking me? You can't just rip me out of school and not tell me what's going on. What the hell is wrong with you?" Then she pulls into Hardy Court, into this parking spot, slams on the brakes and says, "What the hell is wrong with you, Sunny? Huh?! What the hell is wrong with you?"

CULLEN. Did she find out about Chris Beatty's / party?

SUNNY. No! So, I'm like, "What are you talking about?" And she says, "Who still sucks their thumb when they are sixteen years old? Who does that?!"

CULLEN. What?

SUNNY. And then she goes, "You are starting therapy. Right now. We're getting to the bottom of this. This is the office of Dr. Joy Youngblood. She's gonna get you to fix this."

CULLEN. She checked you out of school to...for a...thumb-sucking intervention?

SUNNY. Yes!

CULLEN. That's what she's worried about?!

SUNNY. I guess!

CULLEN. That's so stupid!

SUNNY. Right?!

CULLEN. Maybe she should address some of the other –

SUNNY. I know!

CULLEN. My mom does the same shit. You know how I do that thing with my eyelid?

SUNNY. The pencil thing?

CULLEN. Yeah. She screams at me every time she sees me doing that. Like, "Something is wrong with you, Cullen Prather Towles! Tell me what in the world makes you do that? You will not do that in my house, no sir. Put that pencil down right now!"

SUNNY. Yet she pays no attention to the fact that –

CULLEN. Right. Like, this is the thing that's wrong. THIS.

SUNNY. So stupid.

CULLEN. So how was it? Did you like her? The therapist?

SUNNY. No. She was asking me all these questions and I just sat there with my mouth shut.

CULLEN. What kind of questions?

SUNNY. Rhetorical questions.

CULLEN. ...

SUNNY. Questions that aren't really questions. When someone is not really asking a question they're just trying to make a point. Like, "You understand that you're sixteen, don't you?"

CULLEN. Ugh.

SUNNY. "It's not normal for sixteen-year-olds to suck their thumbs, is it?"

CULLEN. She sounds like a bitch.

SUNNY. Oh, she did ask one real question: "What if someone wants to kiss you?"

CULLEN. Really?!

SUNNY. Yeah. And since that was an actual question, I answered her.

CULLEN. What did you say?

SUNNY. I said, "I'll take it out."

> (**SUNNY** *and* **CULLEN** *laugh a little.* **SUNNY,** *without thinking, puts her thumb in her mouth.* **CULLEN** *looks at* **SUNNY.** *She takes her*

thumb out of her mouth. **CULLEN** *leans in and kisses her.)*

(Beat.)

I can't talk to you next week.

CULLEN. Please tell me you're not –

SUNNY. It's fun!

CULLEN. How is that fun?

SUNNY. We dress crazy and do dances and get to act stupid. It's me and my best friends, like, cracking up together all week.

CULLEN. You can't talk to me?

SUNNY. Nope.

CULLEN. We can't sneak a text or –

SUNNY. Nothing. Nada. You study for your Grabowski test?

CULLEN. Sunny.

SUNNY. I'm just asking!

CULLEN. Yes. Yes, I studied.

SUNNY. Good.

CULLEN. I don't know why, I'm gonna fail it anyway.

SUNNY. Don't say that.

CULLEN. Shouldn't even take it.

SUNNY. You can't just keep skipping. You think you're just gonna be able to keep skipping classes and then magically get handed a high-school diploma?

CULLEN. Is that a rhetorical question?

(SUNNY smiles.)

SUNNY. Take the test. You'll do great.

CULLEN. Can I wave to you in the hall at least?

SUNNY. You can. But I'll get a point ripped out.

CULLEN. Jesus.

SUNNY. Go ahead. Wave. I'll wave back. It's totally worth it.

CULLEN. Aww, that's so sweet.

SUNNY. Isn't it?

(A small kiss. The bell rings.)

SUNNY. Go kill that test.

*(**CULLEN** heads off, **SUNNY** yells after him.)*

You got this!

Scene Three

(**NAOMI** *is sleeping in her darkened bedroom. A few moments of her rhythmic breathing and then the door flies open and* **JULIE** *blows a bullhorn. With her is* **MANDY**, *who has her arm wrapped around a pajama-clad, bleary-eyed, smiling* **SUNNY**. **M.K.**, **DE'SHAY**, *and* **NATALIE** *have their arms around a just-woken-up* **EMILY**. **SUNNY** *and* **EMILY** *are both wearing cow hats and have "point-books" hanging around their necks.*)

(*The bullhorn is so loud. After it sounds, screaming begins.*)

JULIE. Rise and shine, hefer!

(**JULIE** *goes to* **NAOMI** *and rips the covers off of her. She puts a cow hat on her head and a point-book around her neck.*)

Look at this fat cow sleeping so soundly! GET UP! Time to go out to pasture!

NAOMI. (*Smiling, maybe a little teary-eyed.*) You're my Big Sis?

JULIE. Of course I am, Girl.

(**NAOMI** *and* **JULIE** *hug and everyone is like, "Awwwwwww."*)

NOW GET UP BITCH TITS! We're going to Waffle House!!

MANDY. And you can't change or brush your teeth!

DE'SHAY. Mooooooooove along hefer!

NAOMI. We're cows? Not Elvises?

NATALIE. Elvis stuff is really expensive.

M.K. Come on, we have to go get the rest of the herd!

NAOMI. Em! Is De'Shay your Big Sis?

EMILY. Yeah.

M.K. I am, too!

NATALIE. Me, too!

DE'SHAY. We get to share her!

EMILY. The three of them are sharing me.

DE'SHAY. We have to go! I gotta wake up my Little Sis, Angela Culveyhouse!

EMILY. They all have other Little Sisters, too.

M.K. Party train!

JULIE. Come on, Naomi. I hope to God you have on pants.

NAOMI. I don't, I just slept in my –

MANDY. Looks like the Waffle House is gonna get some ass today!

DE'SHAY. Oh my god, yes!

SUNNY. Naomi, this is hilarious!

NAOMI. I can't believe this! I have to go to Waffle House in my underwear?! Oh my God!

MANDY. This is freaking awesome.

NATALIE. Best. Day. Ever.

> *(The girls, hugging each other and cracking up, head out to Waffle House.)*

Scene Four

(**CULLEN** *and* **SETH** *sit in the empty football field.*)

SETH. Man, come on. Just do the extra credit and see if he can –

CULLEN. That extra credit is a joke.

SETH. So, you're just gonna flunk out?

CULLEN. I'm not gonna flunk out.

SETH. Uh, yeah. You are.

CULLEN. It doesn't matter, anyway. You know? None of this matters.

SETH. If you flunk out of high school, it's gonna matter.

CULLEN. I'm not gonna flunk out.

SETH. You're gonna drop out? That's the deal? You're not gonna flunk out, you're gonna drop out? Cool, man. That's super cool.

CULLEN. Shut up.

SETH. Dude. So stupid, here comes the herd.

(*A group of girls is heard "Moo-ing" in the distance.*)

Why is Sunny doing it?

CULLEN. 'Cause everybody else is. It's high school. That's the deal. You do whatever everybody else does. Buy into the bullshit classes, rush a "sorority," play football, learn stupid songs on the guitar.

SETH. It's not a stupid song, it's a classic. And I'm really good at playing it now.

CULLEN. We're all a bunch of sheep.

(*"Moo" is heard again.*)

Nah, man. We're cows.

SETH. Don't drop out of high school. You'll regret it.

CULLEN. None of it matters, Seth. You know that, right? None of this actually matters.

   (CULLEN heads off.)

SETH. *(To himself.)* It might.

Scene Five

> (**SUNNY**, **NAOMI**, *and* **EMILY** *are huddled in the park, wearing cow costumes. They have snuck away from initiation for a pow wow. They have greasy hair, no makeup, and point-books hang around their necks. In the background we can hear initiation games being played.*)

NATALIE. *(Offstage.)* Round and round and round she goes! Keep spinning, hefer!

EMILY. He wouldn't let me leave the table.

NAOMI. I freaking hate your stepdad.

EMILY. He looked at me and said, "Nothing is more important than respect, Emily."

SUNNY. Respect? Bob's gonna talk to you about respect?

EMILY. "And you know how you get respect from others? By respecting yourself."

NAOMI. I disagree.

EMILY. "And this, this parading around looking ridiculous and letting these girls control you, this is not a sign of self-respect."

M.K. *(Offstage.)* We are the Seniors!

NATALIE, JULIE, MANDY & DE'SHAY. *(Offstage.)* We are the Seniors!

M.K. *(Offstage.)* The mighty mighty Seniors!

SUNNY. So, now he's trying to be a good guy? He should have tried that –

NAOMI. They're gonna see that we're not there. Come on, let's get back.

EMILY. It made me feel really bad.

NAOMI. Em, I can't believe you are even listening to a word that comes out of Bob's mouth. He's been awful to you. He's been awful to your brothers. He treats your mom like –

SUNNY. Nay –

NAOMI. What? It's like, you're having fun, you're doing something that makes you happy and you're gonna let Bob make you feel bad about it?

EMILY. This isn't making me happy.

SUNNY. What?

EMILY. I don't like this. I don't like being screamed at and made fun of and forced to sing "Push It" by Salt-N-Pepa at the top of my lungs outside the Special Needs classroom.

NAOMI. Lighten up. It's just initiation.

EMILY. To what? Like, what do we actually get if we go through with this?

NAOMI. We get memories that will last a lifetime.

MANDY. *(Offstage.)* I didn't say stop! Keep jumping you fat cow! One, two, three, four...

EMILY. Memories of dissected pig fetuses being thrown at us? Memories of my stepdad, the worst human on planet Earth, actually making me feel like scum?

NAOMI. That's his –

EMILY. No. It's not. He's right. And I can't let him be right. I can't actually be doing the thing he's accusing me of doing.

NAOMI. And what's that?

EMILY. Having no self-respect!

NAOMI. Don't take yourself so seriously!

EMILY. Nay. I have to take myself seriously. Nobody else does, so I have to.

NAOMI. I'm really not trying to hear you whine.

SUNNY. Nay!

NAOMI. She's whining! Whining is not something I'm interested in! Go ahead! Do whatever you want. I'll be the idiot who doesn't respect herself and goes along with these "awful girls" who just so happen to be our BEST FRIENDS. Fine. So, if I keep doing this, then I'm just a dishrag who doesn't care how stupid she looks?

I'm just an idiot who does whatever anybody tells me to? Okay. Cool. Thanks, Em. I feel great. Thanks a lot.

(**NAOMI** *storms off.*)

EMILY. Her mom's tumor is malignant.

SUNNY. Oh shit.

EMILY. Nay's Aunt Cindy told my mom last night at Zumba. She said that the two of us should know. So that we could be there for her.

DE'SHAY. *(Offstage.)* That's right! Put the whole bag in your mouth! The whole thing!

SUNNY. Is it...like...how bad? Do you know? Did Aunt Cindy say?

EMILY. It's bad. It's really sad.

SUNNY. Oh God.

DE'SHAY. *(Offstage.)* I don't care, stuff it in there!

EMILY. Sunny. I want to quit.

SUNNY. Em.

EMILY. It doesn't feel like...it doesn't feel like these girls are my friends.

SUNNY. They are.

JULIE. *(Offstage.)* Good job! See? That is how it's done!

SUNNY. You know what's weird? I'm actually excited about – like, I'm looking forward to – Rat Court. I daydream about it.

EMILY. About all of them yelling at you?

SUNNY. Mostly it's them yelling at me about Chris Beatty's party.

EMILY. Like...about how you got real drunk?

SUNNY. Yeah.

EMILY. You're looking forward to that?

SUNNY. ...Yeah.

EMILY. Huh. God...the stuff that they could yell at me... about Bob...my family...

SUNNY. They wouldn't do that.

M.K. *(Offstage.)* Where's Emily?

DE'SHAY. *(Offstage.)* Emily?

M.K. *(Offstage.)* Our Little Sister. The girl we share with Natalie. EMILY!!

MANDY. *(Offstage.)* Wait, Sunny...SUNNY!

SUNNY. Come on. Let's go –

EMILY. I don't think this is my group. This isn't my group.

SUNNY. It is, Em. It's gonna be fine, Em. Come on!

> (**EMILY** *and* **SUNNY** *run back to the initiation in the park.*)

Scene Six

> (**CULLEN** *and* **SETH** *are smoking a joint,*
> *listening to Jimi Hendrix on vinyl* *at*
> **CULLEN**'s *house. His mom isn't home because*
> *his mom is never home.*)

SETH. He left his entire record collection?

CULLEN. Yeah.

SETH. *(Pulling an Allman Brothers record off a shelf.)* This is a classic!

CULLEN. I guess that was the trade-off: "You and your mom can have all my old records and I don't ever have to pay child support, or you know, see you again."

> (*Quiet.* **SETH** *practices "All Along the Watchtower" on his leg.* *)*

SETH. Does your mom...she knows you're flunking, right?

CULLEN. My mom could give a shit. All she notices are the little things that don't mean anything. And I'm not in the mood for another "Be Cool Stay In School" lecture, man.

SETH. I just...it matters. This stuff, high school, decisions... we're like real people now. We're like...who we are.

CULLEN. You're stoned.

SETH. I just think, I know shit is hard, but don't you wanna beat it? Don't you wanna get out of this house and this town and... I mean, what does Sunny say? Is she on you about it?

---

*A license to produce *Rat Court* does not include a performance license for any Jimi Hendrix song or any version of "All Along the Watchtower." The publisher and author suggest that the licensee contact ASCAP or BMI to ascertain the music publisher and contact such music publisher to license or acquire permission for performance of the songs. If a license or permission is unattainable for a Jimi Hendrix song, including "All Along the Watchtower," the licensee may not use these songs in *Rat Court* but may create an original composition in a similar style or use a similar song in the public domain. For further information, please see Music Use Note on page 3.

CULLEN. Right now all she's on is a trip with all this initiation crap. But...yeah. She's worried, I guess.

SETH. You're in love with her, yeah?

CULLEN. *(Beat.)* Yeah.

SETH. It's really nice, yeah?

CULLEN. Yeah. Sunny's the best.

SETH. Your mom and dad might not care, but she does. That should make you wanna –

CULLEN. Dude.

SETH. Sorry. Just, doesn't she make you want to...be better?

(**CULLEN** *looks at* **SETH.** *He takes a final pull of the joint. He exhales and he realizes, "Yeah. She does."*)

Scene Seven

(A parking lot.)

DE'SHAY. Angela just told me. That's exactly what she said.

NATALIE. It's coming from Emily?

DE'SHAY. She thinks it's stupid and is trying to pressure the other girls to drop out.

MANDY. What about Sunny?

DE'SHAY. She didn't say, but you know Em and Sunny are best friends.

JULIE. There's no way Naomi is dropping out. She's, like, my best friend. She would tell me.

DE'SHAY. I thought the same thing about Emily.

M.K. That you were best friends?

DE'SHAY. Yeah.

M.K. Then why didn't you pick her to be your Little Sister?

DE'SHAY. I did!

M.K. No, we're sharing Emily because nobody wanted her.

DE'SHAY. She's one of my best friends.

M.K. Dee.

DE'SHAY. So, it's my fault that she wants to quit? Because I didn't pick her?

M.K. No. I'm just saying...you're not best friends.

DE'SHAY. Are you trying to fight with me, M.K.? Is that what's going on right now?

M.K. No, I'm just saying –

NATALIE. None of us need to be fighting. When our bond weakens, Emily grows in strength.

MANDY. I don't like this. This plotting.

DE'SHAY. Angela said she was talking about how stupid she felt, how she didn't want to do Tregg or Rat Court.

MANDY. No one wants to do those things! You think anybody wants to get eggs and trash smashed on them? Do you think anyone wants to sit blindfolded while a group of older girls yells every single horrible thing they can think of at them?

JULIA. My Rat Court was horrible. They yelled about me getting my period all over Rob Hasty's white couch.

NATALIE. How did they even know about that?

JULIA. I don't know! I flipped the cushions!

MANDY. The point is NO ONE WANTS TO GO THROUGH THESE THINGS. But you HAVE to. You have to go through it. That's why you do it.

M.K. To...go through it?

MANDY. Yes! You go through that and...I don't know. There's gonna be garbage thrown at you and people yelling at you your whole life long. You go through this, initiation week, and it can be fun. You get it out of the way and pretend like it's fun. Then, you know...you can do that the rest of your life. Just laugh and get through it.

NATALIE. That's right. Sack up. Every single boy in the world who has grown into an actual man got the shit kicked out of him at some point. Then he had to prove that he could get up and keep going. This is the same thing.

DE'SHAY. Hell yeah. Look at us. We could tough it out. And here we are. Standing strong.

> *(Sort of an awkward silence. Basically, this group of young women don't look like they're "standing strong.")*

Scene Eight

SETH. Sunny!

> (**SUNNY**, *in a crazy outfit – like, truly crazy – turns and gives a little nod. All of her lines in this scene are indicated, but not spoken aloud.*)

Ugh. So you really can't talk to me?

SUNNY. (No. I really can't.)

SETH. Listen, Cullen skipped Grabowski again this morning.

SUNNY. (What?!)

SETH. And Jason Blacklidge told me that he missed all week of Mrs. Watson's class. And like, sixty times before that.

SUNNY. (Are you serious?)

SETH. Just...like, I think he... It seems like he's not gonna graduate. I think he's pretty much...dropped out.

SUNNY. (Oh my God.)

SETH. You're still not gonna talk? This is a big deal.

SUNNY. (I know!)

SETH. Okay, cool. So, we're just gonna not talk about it. Cool.

SUNNY. (I CAN'T TALK!)

SETH. When is this over, this initiation?

SUNNY. (Next week.)

SETH. Okay. Um...is Emily still hooking up with that guy from the mall? That tall dude who works at Chick-fil-A?

SUNNY. (No. He has demons.)

SETH. Cool. Could you say that... I don't know. Could you say that I said, "Hey."

SUNNY. (I didn't know you liked her!)

SETH. Since the ninth grade! You knew that!

SUNNY. (I did not!)

SETH. I've always liked her. I tried to, you know, talk to her that week we were all partying at La Quinta.

SUNNY. (That was a tough week for her.)

SETH. She just... I don't know, never seemed interested.

SUNNY. (Like I said, that was a really bad week for her. Next time you see her you should totally pull out the guitar and start playing "All Along the Watchtower." You're really good at it. She'll like that.)

SETH. Okay. Thanks. Look, it's your life, but...why are you even doing this?

SUNNY. (Because.)

SETH. You don't need to get tortured by older girls just to prove that you're part of a group. To prove that you're like, a person with a life. You're already a person, Sunny. You don't need this.

SUNNY. (Thanks. Tell Cullen that he can't drop out of high school.)

SETH. Alright. I'll see ya.

> (**SETH** *walks away.* **SUNNY** *looks down at her outfit.*)

Scene Nine

(NAOMI, SUNNY, and EMILY sit blindfolded with MANDY, NATALIE, DE'SHAY, JULIE, and M.K. surrounding them. MANDY tightens SUNNY's blindfold.)

NATALIE. All good?

MANDY. Yup.

NATALIE. So. There's been some talk. Some of y'all want out. Some of y'all think this is stupid. That you're too good for this. That right? Y'all been talking behind our backs?

MANDY. When you say you're too good for this, what does that say about us? About those of us who went through this exact same thing? That we're stupid? That we were just losers who went through this?

JULIE. Went through this and loved every second of it.

M.K. Rush week was the best damn week of my life.

DE'SHAY. Trust. That's what this is about. We trusted y'all enough to make you our Little Sisters. To buy costumes for you. Notepads. Presents with your name written on them. Picture frames. Sweatshirts. Really cute stuff.

NATALIE. And that means nothing? You're too good for that?

MANDY. You're not too good for anything. Life is gonna teach you that over and over again. What we're trying to do is teach you that early. And we are trying to make your stupid faces smile while you learn.

M.K. We thought this was about friendship.

DE'SHAY. And respect.

NATALIE. When we say jump, you should say, "How high?"

JULIE. We're not here to coddle you. We don't want to treat you like a bunch of babies.

MANDY. Because you've shown us that you're not babies. Yeah, you might still suck your thumb but you're old enough to get wasted at Chris Beatty's party.

(**SUNNY** *laughs. But she's scared.*)

DE'SHAY. You're old enough to run away to a trashy hotel for a week to hide from your stepdad.

(**EMILY***'s face falls.*)

NATALIE. To hide from your stepdad or to party? I don't know because I heard there was some partying happening in that particular room at La Quinta Inn.

SUNNY. She wasn't there to party.

NATALIE. Oh, did I say talk?

M.K. No, Natalie, you did not.

NATALIE. You don't get to talk. All you get to do is sit there and thank your lucky stars that you even get to be in the same room as us.

SUNNY. We're in a park, actually.

NATALIE. Excuse me?!

SUNNY. We're not in a room. We're in a park. Emily.

MANDY. Oh, really, Sunny? Really?

(**SUNNY** *takes off her blindfold and goes to a crying* **EMILY**. *She undoes her blindfold. She talks to her, very softly.*)

SUNNY. Let's go. Come on. I'll go with you. Let's go.

NATALIE. Are you kidding me?

MANDY. Sunny, don't you dare.

JULIE. This isn't happening.

SUNNY. They can't do this. We're already people. We're good. Just stand up and let's walk away.

(**EMILY** *continues to cry,* **SUNNY** *helps her to her feet.*)

M.K. So, you're gonna just leave?

DE'SHAY. Just walk away?

NAOMI. (*Blindfolded.*) Wait. What's going on?

JULIE. Your two little friends are leaving. You gonna go with them? You wanna be like them and just quit?

NAOMI. …

MANDY. I can't believe this.

NATALIE. *(Calling out to* **SUNNY** *and* **EMILY.***)* You can never come back! You know that, right? This is it?

JULIE. You gonna quit too?

NAOMI. No.

JULIE. You sure??

NAOMI. Yes.

JULIE. Good.

M.K. Did they really just walk away?

DE'SHAY. They can't just do that. They can't just leave.

MANDY. Forget it. They're gone. They're gone for good.

Scene Ten

(**SUNNY** *and* **CULLEN** *sit in the football field.*
SUNNY *has on normal clothes, has showered,*
etc.)

SUNNY. And then they started screaming at her about her
stepdad, you know, Bob.

CULLEN. What were they saying?

SUNNY. About when Em had to take off when things got
really bad.

CULLEN. That week at La Quinta?

SUNNY. Yeah.

CULLEN. That was a fun week.

SUNNY. It was also really sad.

CULLEN. Yeah. Both.

SUNNY. They were screaming and Em couldn't quit crying.
I could hear her. And I was like, "What am I doing?
Why am I doing this?"

CULLEN. And?

SUNNY. I don't know. I just couldn't take her crying like
that. So, that was it. We walked away.

CULLEN. It'll all blow over. You'll all be best friends in like,
a month.

SUNNY. I don't know. This feels huge.

CULLEN. Nothing is huge. We're in high school. Nothing is
actually huge.

SUNNY. That's not true.

CULLEN. It is.

SUNNY. We're already people. It's already happening.

CULLEN. What is?

SUNNY. ...Life.

(**CULLEN** *lies back on the grass.*)

If you don't graduate...if you drop out of high school...
I'm...gonna be really mad.

CULLEN. Sunny.

SUNNY. Doesn't that matter?

CULLEN. Yeah, but it's my life.

SUNNY. We're together.

CULLEN. Yeah.

SUNNY. So. It's my life too.

(**CULLEN** *sits up. He looks at her for a while.*)

CULLEN. You'll be mad?

SUNNY. Yeah.

CULLEN. My mom isn't. My dad isn't. They don't care.

SUNNY. Well. I do.

CULLEN. …

SUNNY. …

CULLEN. Okay.

SUNNY. Okay, what?

CULLEN. I'll go talk to Grabowski. I'll make an appointment with the guidance counselor, see what I can do.

SUNNY. Yeah?

CULLEN. Yeah.

I'm proud of you.

SUNNY. Huh?

CULLEN. All of this…initiation, standing up for yourself, standing up for your friend…giving a damn about me. I'm proud to know you. I always will be.

(**SUNNY** *kisses* **CULLEN.**)

Who are you? Making me feel like I gotta do good?

SUNNY. I want you to live up to your potential.

CULLEN. Making me feel like I have potential?

SUNNY. You do!

CULLEN. Who do you think you are? Huh? Making me feel like…you make me feel like I have a shot.

SUNNY. You do.

CULLEN. Just who do you think you are, Sunny?

SUNNY. You do! You have a shot!

CULLEN. Yeah?

SUNNY. Yeah.

CULLEN. Well. You do, too.

> *(They smile at one another. They lie back on the grass. Under the bleachers of the football field, we can hear* **SETH** *begin to play "All Along the Watchtower."* *)*

EMILY. *(Offstage.)* Awesome. This is one of my favorite songs.

SETH. *(Offstage.)* Really? Cool, I just started messing around. You know, learning to play it.

> *(He continues to play.)*
>
> *(The lights fade.)*

End of Play

---

*A license to produce *Rat Court* does not include a performance license for "All Along the Watchtower." The publisher and author suggest that the licensee contact ASCAP or BMI to ascertain the music publisher and contact such music publisher to license or acquire permission for performance of the song. If a license or permission is unattainable for "All Along the Watchtower," the licensee may not use the song in *Rat Court* but may create an original composition in a similar style or use a similar song in the public domain. For further information, please see Music Use Note on page 3.

TILDA SWINTON BETRAYED US

A. Rey Pamatmat

TILDA SWINTON BETRAYED US premiered May 13, 2017 at the Lion Theatre at Theatre Row in New York City. The performance was directed by Zi Alikhan. The cast was as follows:

LENA	Sadie Parker
MAD	Natalya Gammon
GABRIEL	Jake Dylan
LIZZIE	Tashi Everett
MURIEL	Saman Bayako
OTTO	Irene Lauren
ISA	Petra Brusilo
MARGARET	Maeve Farrell
MASON	Craig Steeley Jr.
ORLANDO	Marina Davey

CHARACTERS

LENA – female, the smart one, any race

MAD – female, the motivated one, a person of color

GABRIEL – any gender, the no-nonsense one, any race

LIZZIE – female, the peacemaking one, white

MURIEL – female, the one in charge, any race

OTTO – any gender, the scared one, white

ISA – female, the earnest one, any race

MARGARET – female, the curt one, any race

MASON – any gender, the real one, a person of color

ORLANDO – any gender, the one who keeps things moving, any race

SETTING

A meeting room in New York City

TIME

December 2016

AUTHOR'S NOTES

The characters can be of any age, but most or all of them are at least over twenty years old.

(Ten chairs. They can be in a line or an arc, but they should all face the audience. In reality, they would be a circle, but this isn't reality, right? This is theatre. Nothing here will be real. Everything here is a metaphor.)

(Right?)

(Across the back of each chair is the name of a character Tilda Swinton played in the following films [these are ordered chronologically, but the actual named chairs can be arranged in the order staging requires]:)

(Lena in Caravaggio *[1986], Queen Elizabeth II in* The Last of England *[1988], Madonna in* The Garden *[1990], Isabella in* Edward II *[1991], Orlando in* Orlando *[1992], Lady Ottoline Morrell in* Wittgenstein *[1993], Muriel Belcher in* Love is the Devil *[1998], Margaret in* The Deep End *[2001], Gabriel in* Constantine *[2005], and Minister Mason in* Snowpiercer *[2013].)*

(Two people enter and stand to one side of the stage. They wear name tags that say, "Hello, my name is: Lena" and "Hello, my name is: Mad(onna)." This isn't cosplay, though, so the bearers of the name tags shouldn't be dressed literally as these characters. They should be dressed like normal people who are mega-fans of Tilda Swinton.)

(Because that's what they are.)

LENA. Just don't go whole hog.

MAD. "Whole hog," Lena? Who says that?

LENA. Shut up, Mad, and listen to the substance of what I'm saying. Go in there. Be rational. DON'T let emotion take over. Then we'll have this war as good as won.

MAD. Yes, good. But it's not a war.

LENA. We're right. That's what it comes down to. So why wouldn't they support us?

MAD. But are we right enough to dissolve the entire organization if we have to?

    (As they go to their seats [under the names "Lena" and "Madonna"], the lights shift.)

    (On the opposite side of the stage two more people enter. They wear name tags that say, "Hello, my name is: Gabriel" and "Hello, my name is: Lizzie." If it needs saying, they are also mega-fans of Tilda Swinton.)

GABRIEL. Just don't bet the farm.

LIZZIE. "Bet the farm," Gabriel? Who says that?

GABRIEL. Shut up, Lizzie, and listen to the substance of what I'm saying. Go in there. Be rational. DON'T let emotion take over. Then we'll have this war as good as won.

LIZZIE. Yes, good. But it's not a war.

GABRIEL. We're right. That's what it comes down to. So why wouldn't they support us?

LIZZIE. But are we right enough to hold the entire organization together if we have to?

    (As they go to their seats [under the names "Gabriel" and "Queen Elizabeth II"], the lights shift.)

    *(MURIEL enters ahead of **ISA, ORLANDO, OTTO, MARGARET,** and **MASON.** They all wear name tags. As **MURIEL** delivers her welcome, the others chit-chat, hug, and find their way to their seats.)*

MURIEL. Welcome to "We Are Tilda, and She is Love" – a community for admirers of British actress, performance artist, filmmaker, and fashion muse, Tilda Swinton. I now call to order our annual summit on this nineteenth day of December, 2016.

Whether you fell in love with her as the queer icon who inspired directors like Derek Jarman and Sally Potter; or as the indie goddess of *We Need to Talk About Kevin* and *Moonrise Kingdom*; or as the gender- and reality-bending creatures of *Constantine* and *The Chronicles of Narnia* you are welcome. We are all welcome here for...

ALL. WE. ARE. TILDA.

> *(Polite applause from the other fans as* **MURIEL** *takes her seat.)*

MURIEL. Our opening tribute is from the 2005 film *Constantine* where Tilda Swinton appeared as the Archangel Gabriel.

> *(***GABRIEL*** *stands and serves up some truly amazing Tilda, embodying their favorite performance by her of all time. Perhaps it's a dance piece inspired by the movie. Whatever it is, stunned silence follows, and then:)*
>
> *(The other fans applaud, wildly.* **GABRIEL** *bows.)*

OTTO. Oh, my god, Gabriel.

ISA. That was so amazing. You're a real talent. You should, I don't know, act or something. For real, I mean. For, you know, audiences – the people!

GABRIEL. Thank you. There's a class of third-graders who would miss me too much if their teacher ran off to Hollywood.

MURIEL. Still, what a thrilling way to kick-off what may be a tough meeting for us all.

MARGARET. Way to bring things down, Muriel.

MASON. Right? Wow.

LENA. I appreciate the honesty.

ORLANDO. Me, too.

LENA. Should we just dispose of the niceties?

ISA. The niceties are...nice. Gabriel's performance?

MURIEL. We'll dispose of nothing.

MARGARET. Instead we'll draw out the torture for as long as possible. Love it.

ORLANDO. We agreed to a standard format for these meetings.

MARGARET. This is a special circumstance. Let's read the letter and get on with it.

ORLANDO. There is a big item on the agenda, but it's only part of the reason we're meeting. Ultimately, we're here to honor and praise the many talents and stunning bone structure of Tilda Swinton...

ALL. We are Tilda.

ORLANDO. ...Not to indulge Margaret's and Lena's impatience.

(*A beat.*)

MARGARET. Fine. Yes. Sorry.

ORLANDO. Muriel?

MURIEL. I sympathize with the desire to rip the bandage off, but let's hear the highlights to remind us, as Orlando said, of why we're ultimately here.

LIZZIE. I second that.

LENA. Of course you do.

(**MAD** *shoots a glare at* **LENA**.)

LIZZIE. I proposed we write the letter about the controversy in the first place. Let's hold off reading it until it's time.

MURIEL. Mason, take us on a tour of Tilda Swinton's 2016.

MASON. Thanks. It's a really great highlights list this year. First, Ms. Swinton played identical twin sisters Thora and Thessaly Thacker in the Coen brothers' *Hail, Caesar!*.

ALL. We are Tilda.

MASON. She produced *Seasons of Quincy*, four short films honoring artist John Berger – one directed by Tilda. The film was supported by the Derek Jarman Film Lab, named in honor of her departed friend.

*(**MAD, ISA, LENA, LIZZIE,** and **OTTO** clap, politely.)*

ALL. We are Tilda.

ISA. May Derek Jarman rest in peace.

MASON. In May, Ms. Swinton starred in her third acting/ producing collaboration with Luca Guadagnino, *A Bigger Splash.*

ALL. We are Tilda.

MASON. Ms. Swinton delivered a tribute to the late David Bowie at the CFDA awards. She eulogized, "Once upon a time you gave us a freak for freaks. Now and forever more, in our missing you, and this is a good thing, you have brought out the freak in everyone."

ALL. We are Tilda.

MASON. For Paris Fashion Week, Charlotte Rampling and Tilda Swinton exhibited their performance installation *Sur-Exposition.*

ALL. We are Tilda.

MASON. In October *OUT Magazine* did a profile of Ms. Swinton where she happily compared being called an "underground superstar" to being like a \ "jumbo shrimp."

ORLANDO. "A jumbo shrimp!" ...Amazing.

ALL. We are Tilda.

MASON. Ms. Swinton shot *Okja*, her second collaboration with Bong Joon-Ho of *Snowpiercer* fame.

ALL. We are Tilda.

MASON. And, finally, following the opening of *Doctor Strange*, December brought us the release of Margaret Cho's and Ms. Swinton's e-mails about her controversial casting in the film. Debates about whitewashing and cultural appropriation were renewed in Hollywood. And here.

LENA. With vigor.

MAD. Amen to that.

ALL. We are Tilda.

MURIEL. Thank you, Mason.

MARGARET. Are we dissolving the club?

OTTO. Margaret!

ISA. We're not... Are we doing \ what?

MARGARET. That's what we're here to find out, aren't we?

OTTO. I don't want to dissolve the club. \ We *are* Tilda.

LENA. Has anyone been talking about dissolving the club?

MURIEL. No one is dissolving anything. No one wants to dissolve anything.

MARGARET. Yet.

LIZZIE. Margaret, seriously, what's your problem?

MARGARET. I don't deal well with change. I know this is not a surprise to anyone. Honestly, I...I love you all so much, and meeting up with you, and Tilda... I couldn't take a slow, painful descent into dissolution. So if we're not all here to do our best to stay together – if we're breaking up, I'd like to –

MASON. Sabotage any chance there might be a positive outcome?

MARGARET. No, that's not –

LENA. If We Are Tilda is going to survive, it will be because we listen to each other and make some changes.

GABRIEL. If anything needs changing.

LENA. Even if it's just that not every film she's in is eligible for the "Tilda Till Dawn Movie Marathon," something will have to –

GABRIEL. We shouldn't assume we'll disband or that things need to change.

LENA. *(Ignoring GABRIEL.)* My point is, Margaret, we need to talk out tough questions, or else the answers will feel wrong whether they are or not. So let's talk them out.

MARGARET. You're right. I'm just not going to talk for the rest of the evening.

LENA. Oh, my god!

ISA. Nobody is saying don't talk. They're saying the opposite.

ORLANDO. Rein it in, everyone. Back to the agenda.

MURIEL. Next up: Isa wrote the letter proposed by Lizzie at our last meeting. We'll hear it and discuss. Isa?

> (**ISA** *stands and produces the aforementioned letter.*)

ISA. Okay, so this is just the rough draft. I'm not, like, speaking for everyone.

ORLANDO. Actually, you are. That's the point.

ISA. No, I mean, if I missed anything –

MURIEL. Isa wrote the letter on our behalf, but we'll take everyone's feedback before sending a final version.

OTTO. Everyone's except Jadis's.

MASON. Otto, come on.

OTTO. I want to know what she'd say.

MASON. Then call her and ask.

ISA. I could e-mail the letter to her –

MURIEL. Jadis knew about today's agenda and hasn't been to a meeting in months. Her absence will be counted as an informed abstention. Isa, please read the letter.

ISA. The rough draft.

MURIEL. Read the draft of the letter.

> (**ISA** *nods and clears her throat.*)

ISA. *(Reading.)* "Dear Ms. Swinton,

"The members of 'We Are Tilda, and She is Love,' a club of your greatest admirers, would like to thank you. We aren't just fans; we're great friends who were brought together because you are such an inspiring, talented, and fierce woman.

"It is with regret, then, that we write angered and betrayed by your participation as The Ancient One in Marvel's *Doctor Strange*. The violent colonization of Asian nations by the West, Hollywood's exploitative cultural appropriation and never-ending depiction of Asia without Asians, and the racist 'Asians are magic, and white people are better at being magical Asians than Asians are' narrative of the film itself are all issues that make us too uncomfortable to support your work.

"As admirers of your bold, powerful, and progressive statements in support of women, queers, people with AIDS, and artists, we were shocked that you closed your mind to criticism from people of Asian descent who deal constantly with invisibility, erasure, and stereotyping in popular culture. However well-meaning your intention in playing this role, the effect was very different and damaging.

"With the President-Elect of the United States coming to power by devaluing the lives of people of color and women, we cannot stay silent. Many of us boycotted the film or requested ticket refunds after confirming how racist the content was. Where refunds weren't furnished, members of 'We Are Tilda' made donations to the Center for Asian American Media in the amount of our ticket costs.

"We are not your enemy. We love you, your work, and your normally forward-thinking politics. We know that you're as human as we are, and that we all make mistakes, so we hope you'll examine the damage you've done in this film.

"Stand with us in the future to fight cultural appropriation, whitewashing, and yellow face in art, on the stage, and onscreen.

"Your still devoted fans,

"We Are Tilda, and She is Love"

> (*Everyone applauds politely, except* **MAD**, *whose hand immediately shoots up.*)

(*Seeing* **MAD**'s *hand.*) Oh, no.

MAD. I just have opinions.

ISA. Angry opinions?

MURIEL. First, let's say good job, Isa. A fine rough draft.

> (*A smattering of applause.*)

LIZZIE. (*To* **MAD**.) Thanks, Isa.

MURIEL. Be specific in your feedback and actually talk about things to add or remove. Orlando will call on people to speak and then ask the group for direct responses before moving on to the next speaker.

> (**MAD**'s *hand shoots back up, along with* **LIZZIE**'s *and* **OTTO**'s.)

ORLANDO. Mad, Lizzie, and then Otto.

MAD. It's too nice.

ORLANDO. Specifics, please, on things to add and remove.

MAD. Okay... Remove half of the, "Ms. Swinton you're awesome," stuff. We're a fan club, obviously we think she's awesome. Add more detail on how *Doctor Strange* is hurtful.

LIZZIE. Everything we discussed last \ time is –

ORLANDO. Show of hands for direct responses to Mad?

> (**LIZZIE** *and* **GABRIEL** *raise their hands.*)

All right, Lizzie.

LIZZIE. Colonialism, cultural appropriation, white supremacist narratives. They're all in the letter.

MAD. But we dance around actually calling it white supremacy.

GABRIEL. Would you prefer, "Dear Grand Wizard of the KKK Tilda Swinton"?

MAD. Tilda took part in the racist re-casting of a role in a white supremacist narrative. Saying it aloud doesn't make it more or less true.

GABRIEL. Tilda Swinton is not a white supremacist.

MARGARET. She just thinks the Tibetan role is better if it's white.

OTTO. Margaret...

MARGARET. Sorry, I forgot I wasn't talking anymore.

MAD. Even if she's not a white supremacist, letting white supremacy happen to get a job isn't exactly awesome.

LENA. Unless you're endorsing Trump's alt-right rule book.

OTTO. But, Lena, "white supremacy" sounds really serious.

LENA. This is serious.

OTTO. It's a movie. I mean, I like how political Tilda is, but really I want to talk about what she's going to wear to the Golden Globes or her next Wes Anderson film or if a *Suspiria* remake is a good idea. Send the letter, but why let it hijack everything that We Are Tilda is?

MAD. The first time I sat in a dark theater watching Tilda Swinton, she was so luminous, so beautiful, and so, so weird. She played the Virgin Mary, showing off baby Jesus as if she were a celebrity on a press tour. And suddenly my weirdness – my queer or androgynous or womanly weirdness was beautiful, too. She made me luminous, film after film. And for a few moments in the dark, I was seen.

And now she's in a film that tells people they don't deserve to be seen. That, as weird as she is, they're too weird even for her. How can I tell people this woman who made me feel seen is the same one telling them they're barely worth seeing at all?

Tilda Swinton should know how personally she hurt us all.

ORLANDO. Gabriel, do you have a response beyond what Lizzie said?

GABRIEL. No, but... The letter says what's wrong with the movie, thoughtfully and respectfully. She's not a member of the KKK. She just made a mistake.

MURIEL. All right, after feedback, we'll vote on making room for a more detailed description of the damage Ms. Swinton inflicted on her fans.

Next concern.

GABRIEL. "Inflicted"?

LIZZIE. Gabriel. Let it go.

(**GABRIEL** *rolls their eyes but is silenced.*)

ORLANDO. Okay. Lizzie, you're next.

LIZZIE. It's too long.

ISA. It could totally be punchier.

LIZZIE. We should cut the President-Elect thing.

(A beat.)

*(**MAD**'s hand inches up.)*

ORLANDO. Hold on. Lizzie, why, precisely, do you want to cut that?

LIZZIE. It's out of left field, and our point comes across without it.

ORLANDO. Okay. Mad, let's... I mean...? Stay civil, please.

MAD. We knew about the whitewashed casting before the election.

LIZZIE. Right. So they're not connected.

MAD. No. The election motivated us to speak, because they are.

LIZZIE. We're sending the letter. Isn't that enough?

LENA. "Enough"? Is that what we're shooting for: the bare minimum?

LIZZIE. We don't have to completely tear her down for one mistake.

LENA. That she still won't admit to.

GABRIEL. Just like you won't admit that really you're mad about the election? And instead of doing anything about that, you're directing your anger at a more available target.

LENA. "Available target"? It's easier to tweet at Trump than it is to write to her.

GABRIEL. She's potentially more open-minded.

LENA. Except after releasing Margaret Cho's e-mails, that's obviously not true.

MAD. Why don't you and Lizzie admit that you're afraid of Trump and you're directing your fear of retaliation at someone else?

GABRIEL. I'm not afraid of Trump.

MAD. You should be.

GABRIEL. I'm afraid that anything short of burning Tilda in effigy isn't enough for you.

MAD. This isn't about satisfying me!

LENA. We need to leave the reference in, because there is a direct connection. Tilda Swinton betrayed us, and we must reject her, because she's basically responsible for Donald Trump.

(*The whole room gasps.*)

ISA. What did you...? \ Oh, my god.

LIZZIE. Tilda is not Trump!

GABRIEL. She is against so much that Trump supports!

LIZZIE. She stood in front of the Kremlin with a rainbow flag to protest the anti-gay propaganda laws!

GABRIEL. Meanwhile, Trump is literally bending over so Puppet Master Pootie Poot can take America up the Trump rump.

LENA. I said she was responsible for him, not that she was him.

GABRIEL. That's completely irrational.

LENA. She's taking advantage of the same system, with the same disregard that –

LIZZIE. We're talking about an *actress* who is in *movies*! Metaphors. Not politics. Not *real* things in the *real* world!!

MAD. Metaphors are real things we use to show how we define the real world.

LIZZIE. She is just. One. ACTRESS!

MAD. And Trump is just one man!

LENA. And this is just one letter!

GABRIEL. And you are just two morons!

MURIEL. OOOKAY.

Lizzie wants to cut the Trump reference; Mad wants to leave it in. We'll vote after we hear from Otto.
YEEEEES...?

> (**LIZZIE**, **GABRIEL**, *and* **LENA** *all look like they're about to say something. Maybe* **MAD** *does, too. After a beat, they all back down.*)

Gabriel, you're on thin ice.

ORLANDO. Otto's feedback on the letter is next. Otto?

OTTO. Okay, look, I don't have a specific reaction to the letter.

ORLANDO. Otto, come on...

OTTO. Hear me out, because – especially after what's going on in this room... This isn't just about an actress. This is about our friendship.

Jadis – my best friend – left We Are Tilda, because of that time Mason showed that Tumblr post from "White Girls with Dreadlocks." Tilda in *The Chronicles of Narnia*?

MASON. And...?

OTTO. There was nothing wrong with what you did, but Jadis didn't feel welcome after that fight.

GABRIEL. Jadis had a point. Tilda wasn't wearing dreadlocks. She was a Highlands woman playing a faerie queen, and the styling was a call-back to her Celtic roots and faerie hair.

MASON. Fine. But "faerie hair" looks like dreadlocks to an American audience. And maybe those movies take place in an imaginary world, but they were made in America for Americans. Someone should have said that whatever they intended, it had a completely different effect. But with all those white producers and white costumers listening to a white actress, there was no one with power to make that reality check.

MARGARET. I mean, it's a world of half-goat people and god lions. Thinking about a non-white audience takes more magical thinking than freaking goat people?

GABRIEL. Stop beating this dead horse. We agreed that effect is as important as intention.

OTTO. And then Jadis left anyway, and I miss sharing We Are Tilda with her, and I don't want this thing with The Ancient One to tear the rest of us apart.

You are my friends, and I love you. You understand why I need to FaceTime you whenever Tilda changes her hair or has a new art installation or is cast as a new woman or celestial being!

But I can't be friends with you if it means letting you be racist. I want We Are Tilda to survive, but if our friendship depends on letting you be racist – if We Are Tilda does – then we can't be friends.

ISA. I love you, Otto.

OTTO. I love you, too.

ISA. I'll be friends with you always, whatever happens.

MASON. I love you, too, Otto, but seriously that is the whitest thing you've ever said.

(The whole group gasps.)

LIZZIE. Mason, what the hell?

MASON. Are we responding now? Because I have a response.

ORLANDO. Clearly, you don't need my go-ahead, so...

MASON. The theater where I work admin is a pretty liberal environment in one of the most liberal cities in the U.S. And you know what I hear day in, day out at work or on Facebook since Trump's election?

"Oh, my god! These stupid, uneducated, poor people in Wisconsin or Michigan or Pennsylvania are so racist. I can't believe them. They're a lost cause. I hope they rot!"

Meanwhile, I look at our mostly white offices, and our mostly white shows. I watch diversity in action that looks a lot more like segregation with "white shows" and "other shows." With mixed-race casts that have a caste system – white leads with actors of color in minor and supporting roles. I watch everyone stress how important it is to not alienate the existing ticket buyers and donors. Basically, to favor rich, white, racist, classist ticket buyers over literally everyone else in America.

And my co-workers wonder why Trump happened? And they think they're too good to associate with THOSE people, because they're so much better and more educated and middle-class and righteous than they are? Because they value black lives and LGBT rights and refugees and women "in their hearts," even if they don't in their workplace or social circles or actual lives?

If I stopped associating with all racists, I would have no co-workers. Or job. Or friends. And there would be no one to check their reality or to push my industry toward actually being the liberal haven it pretends to be.

Otto, you didn't stop being friends with Jadis because she was racist. You stopped because you think you're better than her, and you're afraid that you aren't. Because unless you've actually had the fight or, at the very least, conversation with her about white girls in dreadlocks, then really you're just hiding from an argument you're afraid you can't win.

> (**OTTO** *bolts up from her seat. She doesn't know whether to stay or go.*)
>
> (*Ten seconds.*)

ORLANDO. Otto, do you...want to respond, or –

OTTO. YES.

Yes, I...

I want to...

I'm sorry.

MASON. We're friends, Otto. We can be friends, even if we disagree.

OTTO. Okay. But I don't disagree with you. You're...you're right.

MURIEL. All right, everyone, unless there's anything else about the letter...? Let's vote.

ORLANDO. The first edit on the table is Mad's: that we should –

MARGARET. I'm sorry. I'm talking again.

MURIEL. Margaret, no one wants you to not talk.

MARGARET. I do, because I'm about to open a can of worms. And I'm still terrified that we won't make it past tonight, despite Mason's lovely speech.

ORLANDO. Is it about the letter?

MARGARET. No, it's about voting. I don't think I can until Mad and Lena make the connection between *Doctor Strange* and the Trump campaign strategy.

GABRIEL. Oh, come on!

MURIEL. Gabriel.

LIZZIE. We already talked about it.

MARGARET. There's something about what Mason just said that made it start to make sense to me, but I could use help connecting the dots.

GABRIEL. The dots of nonsense?

MARGARET. It's up to each of us to decide whether or not it's nonsense, isn't it?

> *(***ISA*** *carefully raises a hand.)*

ISA. If I could…

ORLANDO. Go ahead, Isa.

ISA. Maybe it sticks out a little – the President-Elect reference? – because I don't fully understand it either. So I second Margaret. If Mad and Lena talk about it, and we keep the reference, it will help me rewrite it.

> *(***ORLANDO*** *turns to* ***MURIEL*** *who looks from* ***MAD*** *and* ***LENA*** *to* ***LIZZIE*** *and* ***GABRIEL.****)*
>
> *(***MURIEL*** *takes a deep breath.)*

MURIEL. Let's hear it.

GABRIEL. This ought to be good.

LENA. Afraid it will be?

ORLANDO. Lena, you raised the subject. Would you like to take it away?

> *(***LENA*** *looks to* ***MAD.*** ***MAD*** *nods to her.* ***LENA*** *stands.)*

LENA. Okay. Here we go…

Tilda Swinton's role in *Doctor Strange* and the presidential campaign of Donald Trump are both outlandish and vile but real things. We don't want to

think they're connected, because we hate Trump, and
we love Tilda.

ISA. We are Tilda.

LENA. Yes, we are. But they are connected.

People are shocked Trump got elected running a
misogynist, racist, and xenophobic campaign, right?

And they want to dismiss his voters as the worst kind
of alt-right, cross-burning, anti-Semitic, Islamaphobic
racist crazies, right?

But those voters claim that they voted with their
wallets, or – in the case of the Rust Belt "Change" Voters
who voted twice for Obama and then for Trump – they
say they voted for a businessman with the expertise to
"fix" the economy and government, right?

MARGARET. Ugh. GOD.

MAD. It's what they say.

MARGARET. I know.

LENA. In other words, Trump voters claim they voted
not *because* of misogyny, racism, and xenophobia;
they voted *in spite* of it. There were bigger fish to fry,
and it was worth ignoring the pussy-grabbing, mass
deporting, inner-city encoding sewage he spewed to fry
those fish, right?

MASON. Well...

LENA. Worth ignoring for those voters. It's racist, but it's
the racism of privilege, not the racism of prejudice.
It's people who think his words aren't that big a deal,
because there's a country to make great again! A
swamp to drain!

So where does this attitude come from? That these
words aren't a big deal, because they won't really affect
people's lives? Where does this belief come from that
ignoring attacks on certain people won't actually cause
them to feel pain or suffer or die?

LIZZIE. Let me guess: Tilda Swinton?

LENA. Tilda. Freaking. Swinton.

Because when she tells stories that Asian mysticism can be taught without Asians, she's saying that the actual Asian people are the thing that doesn't matter. When she tells stories where the role of Asia and Asians is to support white people in stealing their magic and becoming better at it than them, she's saying the Asian people don't matter or, at least, matter less. Just like the plays in Mason's theatre seasons.

MASON. Amen.

LENA. And outside of the film story, when she says it's okay to erase an Asian character so the scarce jobs for Asian actors are even scarcer, she's telling you jobs for people of color don't matter.

And when she tells you there's still one strong Asian role even though that role is actually in service to the white protagonist, she's telling you people of color don't matter.

And when she supports a director who says he can't create a powerful, Asian woman that isn't a Dragon Lady stereotype and sex object – as though that's a fault of powerful, Asian women and not his lack of skill in writing well-rounded women of color – then she's telling you people of color don't matter.

And when she says all these white people are right about race despite the overwhelming amount of people of color telling her they're wrong, she's telling you the white voices mean more and the voices of the people of color don't matter.

And so, it's okay to ignore the worries of certain people and to vote for Donald Trump. Tilda and Marvel Studios and the Oscars and the stories we tell over and over and over again tell you that not all of our lives matter. People of color, women, and queers matter less. We'll still have good movies and government without them.

AND THAT'S RIDICULOUS.

And that's why we need to send this letter.

(**LENA** *sits.*)

(*Ten seconds.*)

(**MARGARET** *starts to clap.* **MASON, ISA,** *and* **MAD** *join her. Soon everyone except for* **LIZZIE** *and* **GABRIEL** *are applauding wildly.*)

OTTO. Oh, my god.

ISA. Oh, my...wow.

MAD. Thank you, Lena!

MARGARET. Yes. Thank you.

(**ISA** *is on the verge of tears.*)

ISA. You guys , I... Oh, my god. I...

MURIEL. Isa, are you okay?

ISA. You guys, I... I can't... I hate Tilda, everyone.

OTTO. No! We are Tilda!

ISA. Then I hate us!

(**ISA** *loses it. Maybe she throws [or kicks] her chair. Maybe she even throws some others. However it happens, she loses it.*)

She betrayed us, and I hate her. I hate her so much I don't know what to do or say. I just hate her! She opened up so many of our minds, and now she's closing hers and ruining it all! I HATE HER.

LIZZIE. Bullshit.

ORLANDO. Lizzie! Language, please.

LIZZIE. No. No. Bullshit! This is bullshit!!

ISA. Oh, shut up, Lizzie!

LIZZIE. You all want We Are Tilda to self-destruct.

MAD. No, we don't.

LIZZIE. You were upset, so I suggested we write a letter, so we could get past this. Why isn't that enough?

LENA. Thanks for being such a big person and doing us that favor.

LIZZIE. That's not what I mean.

MAD. All you care about is getting this letter right "enough" so we shut up. Because then you'll be able to hide in your sheltered, tiny corner and never talk about racism again. Well, you don't get to do that!

LIZZIE. And you don't get to kill We Are Tilda!

MAD. No one *wants* to kill We Are Tilda!

But maybe we *have* to.

LOOK AT US: a bunch of Americans from all different backgrounds worshipping a white, British woman – an alabaster queen. Fine: we're not here *because* she's white. We're here because Tilda Swinton is an unearthly talent.

ALL. We are Tilda.

MAD. But her talent doesn't give her a free pass, especially if she claims to be all about social justice. And especially, ESPECIALLY since it's weird enough that I spend all my free time praising a white lady. I'm not going to praise her when she uses her whiteness to hurt people!

LIZZIE. So we drag her through the mud?

LENA. We're not slandering her to the press!

LIZZIE. And then we never speak to each other again, because you have self-hatred issues that flare up when you celebrate a white woman?

MAD. "Self-hatred"?!

LIZZIE. You're insecure, so it bothers you when she acts white!

MAD. Racism isn't inherent to "acting" or being white!

LIZZIE. You think it is.

MAD. No, I don't.

LIZZIE. Yes, you do!

MAD. I don't, Lizzie! DO YOU?

LIZZIE. Shut up.

MAD. Do you think you're unable to not be racist just because you're white?

LIZZIE. SOMETIMES.

LENA. What \ the...?

LIZZIE. I mean, no! I mean, I don't know!!

I MEAN...

Aren't I?

If we're in America, and it was built on white racism, and I'm white, and I don't just give away everything I have, aren't I racist? That's what you want: for me to give up everything, for me to have nothing, NOT EVEN MY TILDA!

GABRIEL. Whoa.

(A beat.)

MAD. Lizzie, I want to love Tilda, like you do, but not blindly. I want to respect her when she deserves it and stand up to her when she's wrong.

LIZZIE. But she's clearly on our side! Most of the time. Why waste our energy fighting her?

MAD. Because if we can't fight the people we love and respect, how can we fight the people lined up to actually destroy us?

People want to take away our healthcare, our reproductive rights, our bodies, our homes, our wages, our ability to use public bathrooms, and so much more. And they don't care if we get tired or sick or beaten or die while they do it. But you won't even stand up to Tilda Swinton who might actually listen to you?

LIZZIE. I don't have the strength, Mad, to stand up to everyone, everywhere all the time. I don't.

Okay?

I want to send the letter and forget it happened.

It's been a whole year of campaigning, canvassing, phone calls, fighting. At the end of it, we were supposed to have a President who would take some of the load off us, not someone who would add to it. But now that it has been added to, I can't fight Tilda Swinton. She's one of my few comforts. Even if I know she's wrong.

I can't.

MAD. Then let me do it for you. You started the letter. I'll finish. And the next time I'm too tired, you fight for me. We'll take turns.

LIZZIE. But what if there is no next time? What if this is the end?

LENA. This can't be the end.

LIZZIE. A lot can happen in four years.

GABRIEL. *(As Tilda Swinton.)* It's only in the face of horror that we truly find our nobler selves. And we can be so noble. They'll bring pain! They'll bring horror. But we will rise again!

MAD. I'm as sure that there will be a next time, Lizzie, as I am that Tilda will one day make us all feel luminous again. We'll make sure of that together.

> *(A beat.)*

LIZZIE. …Okay. Please. You finish the letter.

MAD. And if there's any backlash, I'll face it for both of us.

LIZZIE. And I'll take my turn. Next time.

> *(**MAD** and **LIZZIE** hug.)*

GABRIEL. And We Are Tilda?

MARGARET. It looks like we're staying together.

GABRIEL. Pending changes?

LENA. Only where things need changing.

> *(**GABRIEL** and **LENA** shake hands.)*

MURIEL. Shall we bring the edits to a vote?

ORLANDO. The first edit is to remove some of the praise and include more specificity regarding our feeling, as a group, of betrayal. Yeas?

> *(**MAD, LENA, ORLANDO, OTTO, MASON, ISA,** and **LIZZIE** raise their hands.)*

Nays?

> *(**GABRIEL** and **MARGARET** raise their hands.)*

Abstentions?

(**MURIEL** *raises her hand.*)

The yeas have it. Mad and Isa will make those edits.

The second edit is to cut the President-Elect reference for brevity. Yeas?

(*No one raises their hand.*)

Okay. I'll assume the nays then, so...abstentions?

(*No one raises their hand.*)

The second edit has failed.

(**MURIEL** *stands.*)

MURIEL. Before we finish the official part of our meeting, I want to thank everyone and to share a thought.

The first time I saw Tilda Swinton was in an obscure indie movie about the painter Francis Bacon. I heard it starred a young Daniel Craig...

Who got naked...

And made out with another man!

HOW COULD I RESIST?

I watched *Love is the Devil* and was overtaken not just by the moody psychological swamp of the film, but also by the sour-faced woman at the bar whose beauty couldn't be hidden no matter how distorted the shot or extreme the lighting. I fell in love with Tilda in that film. And with the paintings of Francis Bacon. With Derek Jacobi who played him. With independent film, queer film, art, fashion, and the world. My mind expanded and expanded – Tilda Swinton opened doors to me I didn't even know existed.

And now the leader of our country wants to shut doors on so many of us.

Our idols will never be perfect. Nor will our co-workers, friends, partners, parents, President or ourselves. But if the perfect is the enemy of the good, then let us at least strive to be good and demand goodness from everyone who wields power, like Tilda.

When we do, it's not just of her that we're making these demands, because...

(**MURIEL** *makes a grand gesture as* **ALL** *stand.*)

ALL. WE ARE TILDA.

MURIEL. The road to salvation begins tonight.

End of Play

AND ACTION

Eleanor Burgess

AND ACTION premiered May 13, 2017 at the Lion Theatre at Theatre Row in New York City. The performance was directed by Julie Kramer. The cast was as follows:

OLIVIA .... Emma Callahan
MIRIAM. .... Rose Hornyak
ASHLEY .... Rachida Williams
CODY .... Malcolm Grant
ROZ .... Roza Chervinsky
EMMA .... Julia Dec
TORI. .... Irene Lauren
JASMINE. .... Marina Davey
DEAN. .... Mohammad Murtaza
MORGAN. .... Josiah Thorpe

CHARACTERS

OLIVIA

MIRIAM

ASHLEY

CODY

ROZ

EMMA

TORI

JASMINE

DEAN

MORGAN

SETTING

Not close enough to a major city.

TIME

The summer before senior year.

AUTHOR'S NOTES

Please think outside the box when casting. These girls don't have to look like the high-school "types" we're used to seeing in the movies. The Ashley, Miriam, Morgan, and Tori roles could be given to boys, if need be.

Scene One

(An attic in a suburban home that's been converted to look like an evil person's lair. There's a window in one corner with a black plastic bag taped over it. Some random old furniture. A folding screen. There's a bare light bulb swinging from the ceiling in one place and a sheet hanging from the ceiling in another place.)

*(**OLIVIA** and **MIRIAM** stand, facing each other. Tense. Both wear heavy makeup, cool clothes.)*

*(When **MIRIAM**'s lines appear in **BOLD**, that indicates that she's doing a bad French accent.)*

OLIVIA. I did everything you asked.

MIRIAM. You have the jewels?

> *(**OLIVIA** reaches into her jacket, pulls out an elaborate [fake] diamond necklace. She holds it out so **MIRIAM** can see.)*

It's funny. I've never actually liked diamonds. Too transparent. I enjoy mystery.

OLIVIA. I brought you what you want. Now hand him over.

MIRIAM. Camille!

> *(**ASHLEY** enters, holding a knife to **CODY**'s throat.)*

OLIVIA. Owen!

CODY. Jane. I'm all right. I knew you'd come back for me.

OLIVIA. Release him. And you get your sparkly baubles.

MIRIAM. Give me my sparkly baubles. And I'll release him.

(**OLIVIA** *throws the necklace onto the floor.*
MIRIAM *smirks, picks it up. She inspects it
carefully. Then she nods to* **ASHLEY.** **ASHLEY**
shoves **CODY** *toward* **OLIVIA.** *She throws her
arms around him.*)

OLIVIA. Cody...

ROZ. *(Offstage.)* CUT!!

(*Everyone relaxes a little bit; they stand more
naturally, fan themselves. A microphone on
a boom, previously hard to see, lowers down
over* **CODY** *and* **OLIVIA**'s *heads, and* **EMMA**
*steps out from behind the folding screen,
wearing headphones and lowering the mic.
She sets it down and stretches her arms.*
ROZ *emerges from behind the screen, a video
camera over her shoulder. Everyone not in
the movie wears noticeably less makeup and
frumpier clothes.*)

His name is *Owen*, Liv.

OLIVIA. Crap!! Owen! You're Owen!

(**TORI** *enters with an open bag of M&M's in
her left hand and an open bag of tortilla
chips in her right. As everyone talks, she
subtly circulates, offering everyone snacks.*)

CODY. I am indeed Owen. That is my moniker. My nom de
film.

ASHLEY. Don't worry about it Olivia, it could've happened
to anyone.

ROZ. Also, Liv, I need more rage in the next take. Like,
pretend Miriam is Mrs. Bookston.

OLIVIA. Got it. *Ooo, yeah. Rage.*

MIRIAM. Roz, while we're stopped – I have a question about
the line "Give me the baubles and I'll release him." Am
I insisting on that because I'm afraid that she'll trick
me on this exchange, or is it more of a power play?

Because I was going with the latter interpretation this time but if you need a variety of takes –

ROZ. The way you did it was perfect. Do it just that way next time. Okay camera's still rolling, we're gonna take it from Liv throwing the necklace. Thank you craft services.

> *(Everyone goes back to their places.* **TORI** *scurries out, picking up a stray piece of trash along the way.)*

EMMA. Olivia you were holding the necklace in your right hand. Perfect. And Ashley, you had the knife, like a little more – like, higher, like, middle of the throat. Yeah, great – jugular angle.

> *(***EMMA** *hoists the boom up in the air. Everyone gets into stiff, action-hero stance.)*

ROZ. Okay quiet on set. Action!

MIRIAM. Give me my sparkly baubles. And I'll release him.

> *(***OLIVIA** *throws the necklace onto the floor.* **MIRIAM** *smirks, picks it up. She inspects it carefully. Then she nods to* **ASHLEY. ASHLEY** *shoves* **CODY** *toward* **OLIVIA.***)*

OLIVIA. Owen!

> *(She throws her arms around him. They hug.)*

MIRIAM. She has your payment too.

> *(***ASHLEY** *pulls a wad of cash out from her cleavage. It gets stuck for a moment.)*

OLIVIA. Keep your money. I'll find my own way to pay for Harvard. Well Camille it sure has been something. But I'm out.

MIRIAM. Have you been paying attention in chemistry Jane? Remember learning about the scientific method? You think you can just say, "I'm out" and walk away. Would you care to test that hypothesis?

OLIVIA. It's too late for your tricks. I called the police.

*(MIRIAM gives an elaborate evil-person laugh.
ASHLEY joins in with her own villain laugh.)*

MIRIAM. You're almost too perfect for this. We're longing for the police to come. You thought we were spelling this jewelry – Ahhhh selling! Se se se.

ROZ. Take it again.

MIRIAM. You're almost too perfect for this. We're longing for the police to come. You thought we were selling this jewelry for money. Oh no.

ROZ. A little more relish, please.

MIRIAM. You're almost too perfect for this. We're longing for the police to come. You thought we were selling this jewelry for money. Oh no. We very much wish to get it all back to its rightful owners.

(MIRIAM opens a drawer, pulls out a plastic bag full of elaborate [fake] jewels. She reaches into the bag – pulls out an exact replica of the necklace OLIVIA gave her.)

OLIVIA. What is that?

MIRIAM. Did you really think we needed your help because you're flexible enough to fit through small windows? Please.

ASHLEY. It's your face on every surveillance video we told you we disabled. Your fingerprints on every safe we said we cleaned.

MIRIAM. The police will come here. They'll find you. They'll arrest you. And they'll give the jewels back to the original owners, all over this town. Every soccer mom and banker's wife. Only, these aren't their real jewels. These are replicas – and on each one is a single stone that's actually a fragile pellet. Easily breakable. Containing a potent chemical weapon.

OLIVIA. You're aiming for the senator...

MIRIAM. And to think. If only you didn't care about this boy, you wouldn't have helped us get her necklace. This is what you idealistic types never understand. Love...is nothing but weakness.

OLIVIA. Maybe it is. Only, I think there's just one thing you forgot.

MIRIAM. Oh really? And what would that be?

OLIVIA. Seriously? This sucks.

ASHLEY. *Olivia.*

MIRIAM. *Amateurs!*

> (**ROZ** *reappears from behind the screen. Everyone relaxes out of their working poses again.*)

ROZ. Are you freaking *kidding* me Liv?? We have to get a clean take, this is our last day with the whole cast.

OLIVIA. Look I am having your back right now. Seriously, does anyone think this dialogue is okay? Like, these have been the most painful ten minutes of my life so far, and I tried waxing my armpits last month.

ROZ. Cut, obviously!

OLIVIA. "Well Camille, it sure has been something." "It's too late for your tricks." "There's just one thing you forgot."

CODY. We can do this the easy way, or the hard way. She could tell you, but then she'd have to kill you.

OLIVIA. Exactly – no one talks like that!

ROZ. That's the style that we're going for, I am riffing on the genre.

> (**TORI** *enters with a bottle of water and brings it to* **ROZ**, *who takes a sip, hands it back, takes it back, takes another sip…* **EMMA** *brings out a binder.*)

EMMA. What do you want me to write for take one?

ROZ. Write down take one, dialogue flub, camerawork was perfect, and Olivia was a pain in the butt.

ASHLEY. Roz, come on, let's all be nice.

EMMA. I think Olivia has a point.

OLIVIA. Thank you!!

EMMA. Yeah, totally. I've always thought that about the dialogue in this script. It's sort of clichéd.

(**TORI** *exits. She comes back on with a makeup palette and begins to circulate, touching up everyone's makeup.*)

ROZ. I am doing a thing, I am doing a whole Shane Black, Quentin Tarantino thing here –

CODY. I have been doing my best to channel Samuel L. Jackson.

(**CODY**'s *comment makes* **OLIVIA** *crack up. They tend to make half their comments for each other's benefit.*)

ROZ. – Where the movie is *aware* of the tropes in other movies and deliberately plays with them.

ASHLEY. Don't we have a lot to get through today? Maybe we should keep moving.

TORI. You know, one thing Tarantino does pretty often is to have characters fight over something tangible, as like a symbol of the power dynamics –

ROZ. PAs don't give advice. Okay?

TORI. Sorry.

MIRIAM. Olivia if you're having trouble giving an authentic line read, one thing I learned when the drama club did a production of *12 Angry Jurors* is that it can be so powerful when your expression goes *against* the words you're saying. Like if your words indicate rage, try saying them with a smile. It turns out so much more memorable.

ROZ. Miriam, for the hundredth time, I will direct the actors, because I am the director.

MIRIAM. No problem, I'm just trying to be helpful. I know some of the people involved with this project have a little less experience with performance and I'm trying to share a bit of what I've learned.

OLIVIA. Maybe I'd have an easier time with the line readings if I wasn't distracted by someone's bad French accent.

MIRIAM. I *said* that my best accent is Spanish, all right, I was incredibly clear about it –

(**JASMINE** *enters from offstage. She's heavily made-up.*)

JASMINE. Excuse me – are we ever getting to my scene? I've been outside for so long that your pathologically weird neighbor thought it was okay to talk to me.

ASHLEY. Oh, Morgan's not weird. He's shy.

ROZ. We can't have a Hispanic villain, that's really inflammatory, we all agreed to stick to the convention of Western European villains, no one gets offended by the idea that there might be evil French people in the world –

CODY. Technically *Spain* is in Western Europe.

(**TORI** *exits. She comes back on with electrical tape and starts touching up the marks on the floor.*)

ROZ. – And Miriam said she could do the accent.

MIRIAM. I said I would stretch myself.

ASHLEY. And I think she's been doing an amazing job.

CODY. Moi aussi, bien sur, c'est vraiment formidable.

(**OLIVIA** *snorts.* **JASMINE** *turns on* **CODY.**)

JASMINE. Oh my God. You're such a nerd. You should have played the sidekick. That would have been way more believable than the heartthrob.

(*A slight, awkward pause.*)

OLIVIA. Also like, why is she telling me the whole plan? Why doesn't she just say, hey, we're going to leave first, bye, and then I get caught with the jewelry? Or just, let me leave, and the cops find the jewelry, and give it back to people, and I don't know that I should stop them so they all die? That would make *so much more sense.*

MIRIAM. See, the way I've always processed that is that it's *so* important to Veronique to have her genius acknowledged. I think no one has ever really *seen* how talented she is, you know, starting with her parents, but even in school, her teachers, her peers, no one has ever really appreciated her abilities and I think she just has this primal *need* to have Jane see that she's the best.

ROZ. That's great Miriam, thank you very much for that. Also we need it for the plot.

CODY. I also have questions about why the European anarchists are carrying out their diabolical plans in a random suburban town, instead of, say, Manhattan.

ROZ. That's the whole thing, it's *Die Hard* in the suburbs. The whole point is no one expects an adventure like this to happen to ordinary people in a boring town, everyone expects big things to happen to cops, and soldiers, but in this story they're happening to an ordinary teenage girl.

TORI. (*Aside, to* **EMMA.**) Hey, is it okay that they're fighting like this?

EMMA. It's fine, Olivia and Roz have been like this since fifth grade.

ASHLEY. Also, remember the senator is on the foreign relations committee and they're about to crack down on anarchists in Western Europe. That's why Veronique's here.

OLIVIA. Wait, when did that happen?

ASHLEY. It's at the beginning of the movie. The breakfast scene.

OLIVIA. Is that the stuff you guys did last week while I was at work?

ASHLEY. We're filming it on Sunday when Claire's mom is free.

JASMINE. If you ever get through *today's* stuff.

EMMA. For what it's worth, I also find the story really confusing.

ROZ. Oh my god. You are such a suck-up. If you want to get on the cheerleading squad that badly, why not just practice more?

EMMA. Maybe because I'm always busy helping my sister make home videos.

ROZ. *They're not home videos.*

> *(There's a knock at the door, then* **DEAN** *pokes his head in, holding a portable landline phone.)*

DEAN. Um, hey, Roz?

ROZ. *What??*

OLIVIA & JASMINE. Hey Dean.

DEAN. Grandma's on the phone for you.

ROZ. Um, can this wait??

DEAN. Not really. She's about to leave for that cruise thing.

ROZ. Okay so have Emma talk to her.

EMMA. I already did this morning.

> *(***ROZ***, embarrassed, takes the phone, heads to the back of the room. As the interaction below unfolds,* **ROZ** *is quietly speaking with her grandmother – we occasionally hear: "Hey Meemaw." "Yeah, it's the camera from Christmas, thanks again for –" "I did write a thank-you card." "It must have gotten lost in the mail.")*

> *(In this section everyone's very casual and sort of goes off on their own.* **ASHLEY** *checks her phone.* **MIRIAM** *digs her script out and studies it.* **TORI***, humming, polishes the camera lens, charges the battery...* **CODY** *watches* **OLIVIA** *and* **DEAN***'s interaction with amusement, maybe making faces at her. It's nothing like a movie.)*

OLIVIA. Hey Dean.

DEAN. Hey Liv.

OLIVIA. You heading back to campus soon?

DEAN. Not too soon. Couple weeks.

OLIVIA. And until then you're just like, what, you're just chilling? You're like, ooo, I'm a big fish in my little, hometown pond?

DEAN. Not really. I have an internship.

JASMINE. *(To* **ASHLEY.***)* Hey, does my makeup look ready?

ASHLEY. Yeah, it's great.

OLIVIA. Nice. That's cool. An internship is really cool.

DEAN. Oh, you haven't had an internship, it's so not.

OLIVIA. Yeah, no, totally. You're so right.

ASHLEY. My mom says the only makeup you need is a smile.

JASMINE. Ugh, of *course* she does. That explains so much about you.

EMMA. Oh my gosh, Dean, I wish you'd seen it, Olivia is *so* good at acting. She's amazing.

DEAN. I sort of doubt it. I saw her and Roz playing dress-up a lot back in the day and they were the least convincing princesses ever.

OLIVIA. Ha ha.

DEAN. You and Tori enjoying spying on the high-school girl experience?

> *(With* **DEAN***'s attention on* **EMMA***,* **OLIVIA** *starts doing elaborate stretches.)*

TORI. Hey we're in high school now!! Rising sophomore means sophomore.

> *(***OLIVIA** *does downward-facing dog and basically sticks her butt in* **DEAN***'s face.)*

DEAN. Getting ready to do a cheer?

OLIVIA. Oh, sorry, I didn't remember you were there. I'm just limbering up for the big fight scene.

JASMINE. And the big kiss scene. Can't *wait* to see you and Cody make out. Soooo many years of pretending to be "just friends" finally brought to a screeching halt!

CODY & OLIVIA. Shut up.

ROZ. *(On the phone.)* Yup. Can't wait to see you too. Yup. Love you too. Yup. Love you. Okay, bye. Byeeee.

> *(Hanging up.)*

> Liv, stop doing splits in front of my brother. Dean, stay out of here. Everybody else – we're back. Marks!

EMMA. Are we going from the top of the scene?

> *(No one wants to go from the top of the scene.)*

ROZ. Nah, I think we basically got it. Plus we're going to cover it again for Liv's close-up, and then for the low-angle on Miriam. And then for the inserts. Let's just go from "just one thing you forgot."

> *(**JASMINE** sighs and heads back offstage.)*

> *(**MIRIAM** picks up the plastic bag full of elaborate jewels, holds out the copy of the necklace **OLIVIA** gave her. **ASHLEY** stands behind her. **OLIVIA** and **CODY** square off against her.)*

Miriam can you cheat out towards the camera?

MIRIAM. You mean downstage? Sure.

ASHLEY. Um, do you know if I was smiling or frowning?

ROZ. It doesn't matter, your face isn't in the shot.

Okay...rolling. Quiet on Set!

And... Action!

OLIVIA. Maybe it is. Only, I think there's just one thing you forgot.

MIRIAM. Oh really? And what would that be?

OLIVIA. It's nighttime.

> *(**OLIVIA** pulls a [very fake] gun out of the back of her waistband, points it at the light bulb, and shoots. It makes a [very fake] Bang!)*

ROZ. Okay, hold. Grip and electrics!

> *(**TORI** runs to the light switches, turns them off. The overhead light bulb goes out and the stage gets darker.)*

Okay...looking good... Actually – wait a minute, there's – there's a shadow thing. Everyone keep your places!!

> *(Everyone stands uncomfortably frozen as **ROZ** comes forward and looks at a shadow on **MIRIAM**'s face. She steps back and adjusts a film lamp positioned near the window to*

fake "moonlight." She steps forward, checks the shadow; steps back, adjusts the lamp...)

CODY. Isn't it sort of weird that movies are so exciting but making movies is so boring?

TORI. You know there are actually some in-camera techniques that let you adjust that –

ROZ. PAs should be seen and not heard.

(TORI shuts up. ROZ steps forward, stares at MIRIAM's face. Steps back, adjusts the sheet...)

OLIVIA. Hey Roz. Why didn't you ask Dean to be in the movie?

ROZ. Because you lose brain cells around him.

(ROZ finishes adjusting the curtain and goes back behind her camera.)

Don't forget to make like you're shielding your eyes from broken glass. And... Action!

(Everyone [at different speeds] reacts as if there's broken glass flying around.)

(And now, a fight scene ensues:)

(OLIVIA sinks to one knee and fires at MIRIAM. MIRIAM dives to the side, crawls behind some furniture.)

OLIVIA. Owen, run!! Let's get out of here!

(OLIVIA and CODY turn and start to run offstage. ASHLEY runs forward and grabs the back of OLIVIA's shirt, spins her elaborately around [and around]. OLIVIA shakes her off, raises the prop gun and aims at ASHLEY –)

(– And ASHLEY does a full spin and a high kick, "kicking" OLIVIA slowly in the hand.)

(In theory, the kick makes OLIVIA's gun go flying – in practice, OLIVIA sort of chucks it in that direction. It skids along the floor and spins offstage.)

(**MIRIAM** *edges her way toward where the gun went flying.*)

(**ASHLEY** *does a full reverse twirl and "kicks"* **OLIVIA** *in the face –* **OLIVIA** *staggers back as if she's been hurt.*)

(**OLIVIA** *takes a step toward* **ASHLEY** *and throws a punch.* **ASHLEY** *does one of those turn-your-face-away-and-make-a-slapping-sound things.*)

(**ASHLEY** *grabs a small table and throws it "at"* **OLIVIA**, *carefully avoiding her.*)

(**OLIVIA** *grabs* **ASHLEY**'s *shirt, fake-punches* **ASHLEY** *in the stomach once, twice, three times.* **ASHLEY** *does that stage-fighting thing where you jump up and down with a curved back as if you're being punched.*)

MIRIAM. **Get her! Get her!!**

(**ASHLEY** *grabs* **OLIVIA**'s *wrist, twists. She throws* **OLIVIA** *to the floor [gently].*)

OLIVIA. Ow!

ASHLEY. Sorry! Oh – shoot – sorry – um. Take that!

(**ASHLEY** *"kicks"* **OLIVIA** *in the stomach two or three times –*)

(*All of this looks totally terrible and unconvincing –*)

(**OLIVIA** *grabs* **ASHLEY**'s *foot and pulls her to the ground.*)

(**OLIVIA** *climbs on top of* **ASHLEY**, *strangles her.*)

(**ASHLEY** *writhes and gurgles [way over-playing it].*)

(**OLIVIA** *is winning.*)

(*Meanwhile,* **MIRIAM** *finds the fake gun – she raises it – takes aim –*)

(**CODY**, *who has crawled back into view, can
see* **MIRIAM**, *can see her about to shoot* **OLIVIA***:*)

CODY. Liv!

OLIVIA. It's Jane!

CODY. Jane!

OLIVIA. Cody –

CODY. Owen!

OLIVIA. No, I mean, Cody – like, you're bleeding.

(*A wide blood stain has, indeed, appeared
on* **CODY***'s shirt.* **CODY** *looks down, begins to
laugh.*)

ROZ. Crap crap crap crap crap.

EMMA. Cut!

ROZ. Only I get to say cut!

EMMA. Okay do you want to cut?

ROZ. Obviously yes! What the heck happened?

EMMA. You're only supposed to trigger the blood packet
after Miriam shoots at Olivia and you dive in front of
the bullet –

CODY. *Obviously* I know that I shouldn't be randomly
bleeding for no reason. I didn't push the button, the
packet must have torn when I was crawling around on
the floor.

ROZ. PA!

EMMA. You *know* her name is Tori.

ROZ. We need a clean shirt.

CODY. And a new ketchup packet.

(**TORI** *rushes in with a duplicate shirt for*
CODY*.* **CODY** *is about to take his shirt off when
he realizes he's in a room full of girls, and he
exits offstage.*)

ROZ. We need a full reset, I want to do the whole scene again.

(*There are some audible groans. People are
not excited about* **ROZ***'s announcement.*)

EMMA. Okay, so – that table is upright... That trash can is full...

> (**TORI** *starts resetting the scene to where it was.*)

ROZ. While we're waiting on art department, I have a few notes.

> (**CODY** *returns.*)

Olivia – what kind of action hero says "ow"? Ashley, what kind of evil henchperson says "sorry"?

ASHLEY. I know I'm really s– I apologize for that.

ROZ. Miriam, thank you for saying the actual words you were supposed to say.

MIRIAM. I appreciate you recognizing that. You know, once you have the experience of learning two and a half hours of lines for *A Midsummer Night's Dream*, memorizing the five to ten pages we shoot every day just doesn't feel like a big challenge.

ROZ. Liv, you're fighting for the fate of the free world. I need you to really sell the punches. These punches should look *vicious*, okay, like – like – vicious. You look like my mom when she's concentrating really hard trying to do dance aerobics.

MIRIAM. Guess that's what you get when you cast an inexperienced person as the lead.

OLIVIA. Are you serious? The problem is *not* with my acting. There is *no way* that anyone thinks that my fist just connected with her stomach!! She is so obviously punching the air, and kicking the ground, my *grandmother* could see it and she's been dead for two months.

ROZ. It's about the angles. We're going to have an insert shot of the kick here, a close-up on your face in pain there, a cut to Owen watching you get hurt. We're going to cut out all the parts that are goofy or imperfect or pedestrian and carefully craft a totally artificial narrative that is way way better than anything that actually happens in real life.

CODY. Ooo pedestrian. Nice word choice.

EMMA. She learned it studying for the SATs. She makes me quiz her every night.

ASHLEY. Really? You're not taking the ACTs?

ROZ. Can we focus please??

> *(Note: the real fights should sound and look totally different from the fake movie fights. Instead of trying to sound cool, and to act angry, the characters are genuinely agitated, struggling more with words. And the ones who aren't speaking, instead of standing there calm and still, posed for the drama, are being awkward: hanging back in the corner, looking away, fidgeting, getting ready to talk and then backing off. Maybe they take refuge in activities: cleaning, eating, checking their phones...)*

CODY. While we're stopped – every once in a while I would really like to throw a punch.

ROZ. No, that's the whole point, I'm reversing gender tropes, and you get the girl's role, you sit there, and you scream, and you say obvious things, and then your death, when you dive in front of a bullet that was aimed at her, motivates our heroine to accomplish her final act of greatness, just like the death of every girl in every movie ever.

CODY. Well it would also kind of reverse gender tropes if I punched a girl.

OLIVIA. Also, it makes *no* sense that Ashley wouldn't change her mind when she realizes this is about international *arms dealing*. Like she went overnight from volleyball captain to supervillain because a foreign exchange student *told* her to?

ASHLEY. Well, remember that scene where she promises to get me off the wait list at NYU if I help? We shot it last week. But that might have been the day you had driver's ed.

OLIVIA. *Arms dealing*, though. Also, if there's all this video footage, why haven't the cops caught them yet? Also, where did I get a gun??

ROZ. And you couldn't have raised any of these issues back before we started shooting?

> (**JASMINE** *enters, dressed in a ridiculous lady-cop uniform.*)

JASMINE. *Are we ever getting to my scene like ever. Ever.* Your super awkward neighbor just brought me *snacks.*

> (*There's a moment while everyone takes in the costume.*)

EMMA. Is that your costume?

JASMINE. It's all that was on Amazon. Apparently impersonating a police officer is like a serious crime, so...

MIRIAM. Is that a stripper's outfit?

ASHLEY. Hey no slut-shaming.

MIRIAM. I'm not slut-shaming, I'm costume-shaming.

JASMINE. Well *I'm* not the one who wore a beret to school for six months because I thought it made me look sophisticated and European.

OLIVIA. You look ridiculous.

JASMINE. More ridiculous than you making out with Cody?

CODY. Yeah, I know, I know, okay, they should have gotten Dean to play the lead, that would be *so* great, you'd get to kiss him, and he wouldn't be all nerdy and *he'd* have been able to climb that wall for that kidnapping scene, and everyone would be so much happier.

OLIVIA. No! Cody, we don't think that. Come on. Of course not.

> (*Somewhere, a phone rings.*)

ROZ. Is that a phone? Did somebody not silence their phone? Like, does someone have so little respect for what we're doing here that on the last possible day that we can get everybody together, after two weeks of getting used to how film sets work, someone *did not bother to silence* *their phone*?? You know Hitchcock said actors should be treated like cattle, and I am really starting to get what he was talking about!!

(**OLIVIA** *puts her arms around* **EMMA** *and* **TORI***'s shoulders.*)

OLIVIA. Emma. Tori. Someday, when you're about to be seniors. With the whole wide world ahead of you, and it's midsummer, and you could be doing whatever you want, and your friend says, hey, let's stay indoors for three weeks making a movie – say no.

ROZ. You know what, I am the director, and I am ordering you to stop giving little clever opinions and to get back to work.

OLIVIA. You can't order me around!

ROZ. Can too!

(**OLIVIA** *picks up the bag of jewelry, strides to the window, opens it, and chucks the bag outside.*)

You are the worst. Look I know that you have no vision, and no real dreams, because you only care about looking cool, and you only agreed to do this so that you could flirt with Dean –

OLIVIA. I agreed to do the movie because we're *friends*, idiot, but I am really regretting that right now because if one minute of this stupid movie ends up on YouTube I will literally drop dead from embarrassment.

(**ROZ**, *deeply upset, runs out of the room.*)

(*A long, awkward pause.*)

JASMINE. Great. Now we're never going to get to my scene.

MIRIAM. Maybe if you were a little more pleasant to work with, you'd have gotten a bigger role.

JASMINE. Please, everyone knows the only reason Roz asked you to do a lead role is because you barely have friends so you have no problem clearing three full weeks of your summer.

ASHLEY. Guys could everyone please just try to be a little nice??

JASMINE. Does it get boring being such a goody two-shoes all the time?

OLIVIA. Jasmine! You are like a relentlessly unpleasant person and you should examine your behavior and think about like – if life were a movie, would you be the bad guy? I think yes.

> *(Beat.)*

JASMINE. Tell Roz I quit. Someone else can be the one to find the bodies.

> *(**JASMINE** leaves.)*

TORI. You know I was *really* excited to help out with making a movie. I thought that sounded so cool. But you guys are all just obsessed with how *you're* coming across and not even trying to make something awesome. I thought seniors were more mature than this!!

> *(**TORI** storms out.)*

EMMA. Well, I guess we can –

> *(She turns the lights on. The girls remove high heels. **ASHLEY**'s still stuck on what Jasmine said)*

ASHLEY. I think it's good to be nice. I know no one wants to be the nice girl, everyone wants to be the hot girl or the smart girl or the funny girl but I am the nice girl and you know what? I think it is good to be the nice girl, I think that's really important, I wish more people tried really hard to be the nice one in their group of friends, I think everyone should be a lot nicer to each other.

CODY. At what point do your menstrual cycles all sync up and we get three weeks in a row of happiness between giant blowout fights?

OLIVIA. You know it actually turns out that periods are when women experience a sudden drop in female hormones, which is what triggers the shedding of the uterine lining, so the way women are when they're PMSing is the way men are *all the time*. True story.

> (**TORI** *comes back in with a broom and starts sweeping.*)

Maybe we should all just go home. Pick this up tomorrow.

MIRIAM. I go to Cincinnati tomorrow.

OLIVIA. What?

MIRIAM. For a week. I'm visiting my dad.

ASHLEY. And then by the time she gets back it's preseason.

OLIVIA. Well that sucks.

> (**DEAN** *enters.*)

DEAN. Um. How exactly did you guys make my sister cry?

> (*The girls look at each other, alarmed.*)

OLIVIA. I'll go talk to her.

EMMA. No, that's okay. I think I should.

> (**EMMA** *goes out with* **DEAN**. *He glares briefly at* **OLIVIA** *before he goes.*)

> (*There is silence.*)

OLIVIA. I didn't mean to upset her. I was just... I was just saying what I think. I didn't mean it.

ASHLEY. Well, you said it. You don't get a do-over.

You always complain about *everything*, Liv.

OLIVIA. No I don't.

MIRIAM. Yeah, you do. You know it is *hard* to do what Roz did. It's hard to create something, and put it out there in the world. It's *a lot* easier to pick things apart. Like when the drama club did our production of *Into the Woods*, the school paper really made fun of my version of the witch's rap, but you know what, I'm a lot more proud to be someone who *tried* something, even if it came out goofy, than someone who just sits back and criticizes and pokes fun.

OLIVIA. Can you just calm down all right?

MIRIAM. Oh I'm sorry, I'm not supposed to have legit opinions, I'm just supposed to be the butt of your jokes. I'm not perfect pretty Olivia, I'm not the star –

CODY. Guys, it's not a movie. It's life. Everyone gets equal screen time. Everyone's the star.

MIRIAM. I'm just saying. If you think everything sucks, why don't you try to figure out how to make it *better*?

(*Beat.*)

OLIVIA. Okay – okay...

Fine. I will.

I will make the ending better.

MIRIAM. Okay.

OLIVIA. Okay.

I will. I'm going to – any minute now – I'm going to have an idea.

TORI. Hey. If you don't mind me speaking up?

It seems like the main problem you mentioned was with the fighting? That and the fact that you couldn't believe Ashley was sticking with the bad guys?

OLIVIA. I don't really like the fact that I die at the end, either. Like I get it, you know, I get why she destroys the necklace in the attic and kills them all so it can't hurt anyone else, but it just seems really...like, bleak. But I don't know how else Jane could get out of it.

TORI. Okay, well – if you were in that situation, how would you solve it?

(**OLIVIA** *draws a total blank.*)

Okay so you're there, and she's over there, and they've got the necklace.

(*People shuffle over to roughly where they stood before.*)

OLIVIA. And I've gotten Owen back. And then you tell me your whole plan about like - you're going to frame me and poison the world.

MIRIAM. **And to think. If only you didn't care about this boy, you wouldn't have helped us get her necklace. This is what you idealistic types never understand. Love...is nothing but weakness.**

> (OLIVIA *runs to get the fake gun. She points it at* MIRIAM.)

CODY. I thought you didn't like the fight scene?

OLIVIA. I'm thinking!!

EMMA. I'll take notes.

> (She starts taking notes on the continuity binder.)

OLIVIA. You know Veronique I'm usually not a big fan of my dad's NRA membership, but I'm making an exception now.

ASHLEY. Oh I don't really like that. I feel like then we're endorsing gun ownership.

CODY. I really feel like we can sort those kinds of details out later.

MIRIAM. **You won't actually shoot us. I know you won't. Camille – disarm her!**

> (ASHLEY *starts toward* OLIVIA, *who backs away.*)

Okay Olivia. What are you going to do?

OLIVIA. I'd – I'd –

I'd try to persuade Camille!

Right – I mean like, she's not a weird French exchange student! She and I go way back, she's been sucked into this weird international terrorism ring too, she must not like it.

ASHLEY. Yeah. That's a good point.

OLIVIA. I'd be like... Hey! Camille! Come on! I know that we've all been through a lot – you know, diamond thefts...rooftop chases. But – come on!

EMMA. I'm not sure I'm getting all of this.

TORI. I can film it!

(She sets up the video camera, starts filming their improvisation.)

OLIVIA. I know you still have...humanity! And – concern for this town, and these people, I mean, this isn't just any senator – it's Katie's mom!! And this will kill her! You don't want that to happen, do you?

MIRIAM. Good. Good. Make it specific. You know they say that the path to universality lies through specificity. Like Grover's Corners in *Our Town*.

OLIVIA. Um...right. So... So...

Remember when we were in kindergarten? And we used to go over to Katie's house? And her mom made like –

ASHLEY. Turtle-shaped pancakes!!

(The girls all start laughing.)

OLIVIA. Yes!!

TORI. Wait what?

OLIVIA. Roz's mom used to make them for all of us! They're like blobs with feet.

EMMA. They're really cute.

OLIVIA. Okay! Okay – remember? Her mom used to make us turtle pancakes? And – and remember that time she took us to D.C.? And we went to the zoo, and saw the elephants?

ASHLEY. Aw, I loved that field trip!

MIRIAM. Stay in character.

ASHLEY. Right – sorry.

OLIVIA. You and me and Cody – Owen – and Roz – we all went – and she got us in to pet the baby hippo! Oh, this sounds so stupid, this would never persuade anyone!

TORI. No, you have to think – there's going to be a close-up of her face – with tears in her eyes –

ASHLEY. Wait, do I have to act? Roz promised I wouldn't have to act and I'd just have to do kickboxing because I know how to do it already.

MIRIAM. You can do it. I can coach you. And we can put eye drops in your eyes for the crying.

TORI. And there'll be cool lighting. And dramatic music –

> (**TORI** *moves the lamp closer to them.* **CODY** *pulls out his phone and puts on some grand, soundtrack-style music.**)

> (*Unseen,* **ROZ** *returns, watches them from the sidelines.*)

OLIVIA. You can't hurt – this whole town, Camille! Sure I know it's boring, I know we're about to graduate, and leave forever, but we've been through so much together – there's good people here –

MIRIAM. Don't listen to her. This town is nothing. These are just ordinary little nothing people, and she's the most nothing of all. Get her!

> (**ASHLEY** *takes a couple steps toward* **OLIVIA**, *who raises her fake gun.*)

OLIVIA. I don't want to hurt you.

CODY. Come on Camille. We're friends.

OLIVIA. ...I won't do it.

TORI. Close-up – she takes her finger off the trigger.

> (**OLIVIA** *takes her finger off the trigger, then lowers the gun.*)

ASHLEY. Then I won't either.

> (*She lowers her knife.*)

MIRIAM. Roz!

OLIVIA. No, it's Camille.

MIRIAM. No, it's *Roz.*

> (*She points. Everyone notices* **ROZ** *watching them.* **EMMA** *stops the music.*)

---

*A license to produce *And Action* does not include a performance license for any third-party or copyrighted music. Licensees should create an original composition or use music in the public domain. For further information, please see Music Use Note on page 3.

OLIVIA. Sorry – we're not – we were just messing around. It was just – stupid – to pass the time while you were busy.

ROZ. No, it's fine. I like it. I mean it's a little sappy, but. It's good.

OLIVIA. It barely changes anything, it's – your whole story is still in place.

MIRIAM. We can still use all of that sleepover heist set piece... Which I'm not sure if I've told you but I really think it's good. Very *Italian Job*.

ROZ. ...So what happens next?

ASHLEY. So we turn on Miriam.

> (**ASHLEY** *and* **OLIVIA** *both turn on* **MIRIAM**.)

OLIVIA. I think we all know who the real enemy is.

MIRIAM. And then I would –

> (**MIRIAM** *reaches down and picks up the diamond necklace, makes to run off with it.*)

Only, obviously this would be the whole bag of jewelry –

> (**OLIVIA**, **CODY**, *and* **ASHLEY** *race after her, stop her.*)
>
> (*They get to a place where* **OLIVIA** *and* **ASHLEY** *are holding* **MIRIAM**'s *arms.*)

OLIVIA. Cody, if you want to get your punch in –

> (**CODY** *winds up* –)

CODY. Ooo, Roz, no, you're right, I totally don't want to hit anyone. Um. So instead I would – um – I would take the necklaces!

> (*He grabs the necklace away from* **MIRIAM**, *holds it carefully.*)
>
> (*They've run out of steam.*)

EMMA. And that's when you hear the siren outside!

ASHLEY. Yes! Only – Jasmine quit. We don't have a police officer.

TORI. Roz – you should do it. Quentin Tarantino always puts himself in his movies.

ROZ. No. Come on. I'm not like them, I can't act. And to be honest I think his cameos are the worst part of his films.

OLIVIA. But we need someone to end the movie.

(**MORGAN** *enters, holding the bag of necklaces.*)

ASHLEY. Morgan!

MORGAN. Um. Hi. Sorry. Um. These. I think these fell out of your window, maybe? I mean, I saw them fall out of your window. I think. So I sort of assumed they were yours. And that you might want them. You know. Since they're yours. The necklaces.

ROZ. Thanks.

(**ROZ** *takes the bag.*)

MORGAN. Um, yeah, so, so Jasmine told me, y'know, not to talk to you guys at all, ever, because you're busy, so I'll be going. Now. Yeah.

ROZ. Hey Morgan... Do you want to be in a movie?

MORGAN. Um. What?

ROZ. We need a police officer for the final scene. Can you help out?

OLIVIA. We're just filming a demo now. But basically all you have to do is come in – you know, as an officer – like, tough.

MORGAN. Um...okay, like...

(**MORGAN** *leaves and comes back in, trying to look tough.*)

ASHLEY. And you see me, holding the bad guy by one arm, and her, holding her by the other –

CODY. I am standing around looking heroic in a nonviolent way.

OLIVIA. And I say – "Officer! Look I know this looks like bad, like really bad, but you have to listen to me, this woman is super *dangerous* –"

(**MORGAN** *does an excellent job turning into a police officer.*)

MORGAN. Well I don't know ma'am. This looks pretty bad –

CODY. But I can back up everything she says –

ROZ. And then she starts to explain – which seems kind of repetitive and anticlimactic.

TORI. Wait! What if there was one more twist?

ROZ. How do you mean?

TORI. What if, Olivia's starting to explain, and the officer goes – I know everything already. Your friend already called and told me the whole story.

ASHLEY. Wait, you mean me? I saved the day?

TORI. I would believe you saving the day.

(*Everyone looks at* **ROZ.**)

OLIVIA. Roz – what do you think?

ROZ. I think that sounds awesome.

(**OLIVIA** *whoops. Some of the girls jump up and down with excitement.*)

MORGAN. You don't have to explain miss. Your friend here already called and filled our precinct in on the whole story.

ROZ. This girl's going away for a long, long time.

OLIVIA. Get out of here Frenchie!!

(**MORGAN** *and* **ASHLEY** *haul* **MIRIAM** *toward the door.* **CODY** *and* **OLIVIA** *are left facing each other in the middle of the stage.*)

And then – and then so I guess – we – we kiss? To celebrate?

(**OLIVIA** *and* **CODY**, *not excited about it, slowly inch toward each other to kiss. It's the least romantic thing ever.*)

ROZ. Why do they have to kiss? What if the whole movie was just about, she shows up to protect her friend? I mean, if I thought any of you were going to *die*, I would fight really hard to keep that from happening even though none of us have made out.

TORI. *Not* having a hookup would be another way to mess with the genre.

CODY. So then we hug!

> (**OLIVIA** *and* **CODY** *share an enthusiastic hug.* **ASHLEY** *high-fives* **MORGAN, MIRIAM.**)

EMMA. But wait – what's the last line? If we got rid of the whole, cop-wondering-how-everybody-died thing – how does it end?

> (*A moment of silence. They all think... Then* **ROZ** *whispers in* **ASHLEY** *and* **OLIVIA**'s *ears.* **OLIVIA** *nods.*)

ASHLEY. But wait. How will you pay for Harvard?

OLIVIA. Well. I just lived through something pretty cool. I was thinking I could sell the rights to our story. But for now, I've got to go home, and study for the SATs!

CODY. Yessssss.

ROZ. It's pretty cheesy.

MORGAN. I like it.

OLIVIA. Do we have an ending?

ROZ. I think we do.

> (*They all group hug.*)

TORI. Aaaaand cut!

End of Play